MW01602595

Highlander's Forbidden Love

Loved by a Highlander

Book 5

by Debra Chapoton

ISBN: 9798861660686

Imprint: Independently published

Follow me for new book releases:
https://www.amazon.com/stores/author/B003MX4NCS

Books by Debra Chapoton

The Highlander's Secret Princess
The Highlander's English Maiden
The Highlander's Hidden Castle
The Highlander's Heart of Stone
The Highlander's Forbidden Love

Second Chance Teacher Romance series written under pen name Marlisa Kriscott (Christian themes):

Aaron After School
Sonia's Secret Someone
Melanie's Match
School's Out
Summer School
The Spanish Tutor
A Novel Thing

Christian Non-fiction:
Guided Prayer Journal for Women
Crossing the Scriptures
35 Lessons from the Book of Psalms
Prayer Journal and Bible Study (general)
Prayer Journal and Bible Study in the Gospels
Teens in the Bible
Moms in the Bible
Animals in the Bible
Old Testament Lessons in the Bible
New Testament Lessons in the Bible

Christian Fiction:
Love Contained
Sheltered
The Guardian's Diary
Exodia
Out of Exodia
Spell of the Shadow Dragon
Curse of the Winter Dragon

Young Adult Novels:
A Soul's Kiss
Edge of Escape
Exodia
Out of Exodia

Here Without A Trace
Sheltered
Spell of the Shadow Dragon
Curse of the Winter Dragon
The Girl in the Time Machine
The Guardian's Diary
The Time Bender
The Time Ender
The Time Pacer
The Time Stopper
To Die Upon a Kiss
A Fault of Graves

Children's Books:
The Secret in the Hidden Cave
Mystery's Grave
Bullies and Bears
A Tick in Time
Bigfoot Day, Ninja Night
Nick Bazebahl and Forbidden Tunnels
Nick Bazebahl and the Cartoon Tunnels
Nick Bazebahl and the Fake Witch Tunnels
Nick Bazebahl and the Mining Tunnels
Nick Bazebahl and the Red Tunnels
Nick Bazebahl and the Wormhole Tunnels
Inspirational Bible Verse Coloring Book
ABC Learn to Read Coloring Book
ABC Learn to Read Spanish Coloring Book
Stained Glass Window Coloring Book
Naughty Cat Dotted Grid Notebook
Cute Puppy Graph Paper Notebook
Easy Sudoku for Kids
101 Mandalas Coloring Book
150 Mandalas Coloring Book
Whimsical Cat Mandalas Coloring Book

Early Readers
The Kindness Parade, The Caring Kids: Spreading Kindness Everywhere
The Colors Of Friendship: The Caring Kids, Embracing Diversity
Believe In Yourself, The Caring Kids: Building Self Esteem
Friends With Fur And Feathers: The Caring Kids, Animal Friends
Celebrations All Year Round: The Caring Kids: Our Special Days
Feelings In Full Color: The Caring Kids: A Guide To Feelings

Non-Fiction:
Brain Power Puzzles (11 volumes)
Building a Log Home in Under a Year
200 Creative Writing Prompts
400 Creative Writing Prompts
Advanced Creative Writing Prompts
Beyond Creative Writing Prompts
300 Plus Teacher Hacks and Tips
How to Blend Families
How to Help Your Child Succeed in School
How to Teach a Foreign Language

Chapter 1

"LOVE'S PATH BE strewn with thorns," Thomas said, as if he, an old cross-eyed bachelor, had secrets to share.

Huey Beldorney smirked and took another swig of cider. He sat at Thomas's well-worn kitchen table and stared at the flames in the small cabin's hearth, rain pounding outside. "And ye ken aboot such things because …?" He let the question hang in the warmed air as a flash of lightning drew their attention to the window.

"I ken more about these things than ye do. I was witness to yer parents' weddin' as they defied their fathers, Laird McKelvey and Baron Beldorney. Yer father was prepared to forego his fortunes and yer mum, Fenella, God rest her soul, was willin' to leave Castle Caladh to rake the bare earth and farm the land with him." He coughed and wiped his mouth on his sleeve. "Aye, love and honor clash like these thunderous storms, they do."

Huey nodded and leaned back in his chair. He'd stopped to check on his father's old friend when he was riding home from Beldorney Hall and the first large drops of October rain hit his feathered cap.

Another sharp crack startled them. Thomas continued, "And yer aunts and uncles … they have stories, too. Ye were but a wee lad when Keir defied tradition and risked a political scandal that mighta sent him to the gallows."

Huey knew a bit of that history. His aunt Eleanor was English and of the royal bloodlines, though no one spoke of it anymore.

1

"I ken what ye're thinkin'." Thomas gave a humming sigh for emphasis. "Ye've had yer eye on the Kilmahew lass, daughter of the eldest brother. Did ye ken that yer Aunt Anabel was meant to marry the youngest Kilmahew brother at one time? Yer Uncle Jack changed that … och, I could tell ye a tale of passion and defiance …"

Huey cocked his head like a curious dog and wondered how the old man was privy to all his family's scandals, for surely it sounded like every McKelvey, his mother included, had a tale of forbidden romance that had been whispered over the windswept moors of Scotland.

Thomas finished his mug and refilled it from a different jug, one with a stronger flavor. He aimed his steady eye at Huey while the weaker one wandered off to the side. "I ken ye willna take the advice of an old man such as I, but I saw ye last summer … I saw ye lettin' yer eyes follow after her. The brown-haired lass, Rhona. Aye? Me advice is that ye look elsewhere. Marry a McDoon or a McDonough or even a Stewart, but stay away from Rhona Kilmahew unless ye want to shatter the ancient bonds o' clans and," he sent both eyes in the direction of the hearth, "ignite the flames o' war."

Huey tried to laugh it off. "Nay, Thomas … ye've got it wrong. I pranced aboot the Highland games like all the other lads. Showin' off our skills. I practiced hard fer the archery contest and I won. I couldna help it if the lass came up to me, now could I?"

Thomas huffed.

"Besides," Huey went on, "all the tales of blood feuds and rivalries are ancient history. We're headin' fer a new century. If I pay a visit to Kilmahew lands … well … I dare say it willna threaten to unravel the delicate fabric of Highland society or customs or clan rules. Now will it?" He tapped his mug with his fingernail. "Besides, I'm quite aware of why my grandfather, Laird McKelvey, hates their gamblin' ways, but that was from time past. They barely took wagers at the games."

"Barely, ye say? Och, yer attention was on the skirts and ye dinnae see their coffers fill with all their shady deals."

"Thomas … let us speak of somethin' else." Huey certainly didn't want Thomas to guess how infatuated he was with the Kilmahew lass. "Do ye think this rain will let up soon?"

***

2

RHONA KILMAHEW WAS devastated. Freedom might echo in the wind and love tiptoe through the heather, but she would never be free and she would never, ever love the man her father just told her she had to marry: Dylan McDoon. Why, the man was practically twice her age. She shivered again at the thought. The man was crass, had married and buried two wives, Orla McHenry and Shona McDonnell, both dead within a year of marriage. Marriage to that man was a death sentence, it seemed.

She sat in her room, fuming, fretting, and brushing her long brown locks all by herself. Grooming her hair was a chore best left to her maid, Mairi, but that poor lass was abed with an ague.

Rhona sighed. Why couldn't she choose who she wanted to spend her life with? She'd had her eye on all the wrong lads, according to her father. He had sent away the stableboy when she, at fourteen, had prepared a secret picnic with him. He forbade the tradesman to bring his son when, at fifteen, Rhona had waved at him.

She sighed again and remembered how a visit to Edinburgh was cut short when she was sixteen. It was her first time in a city and she was enamored of the sights and sounds and the handsome young men marching through the streets acting as if they were a real militia. She smiled at one and he smiled back. Her father pulled her forcefully away from the carriage window. She was more careful the next year and the next, but this past summer, at the Highland games held once again on McKelvey lands, she'd fallen fast and hard for the handsome archer. She didn't know his name until the Laird announced him as his grandson, Hubert Beldorney.

"Ah," she sighed aloud. "Huey Beldorney."

What a misfortune that she'd been born in a land where love was bound by the shackles of tradition. Her heart yearned for a man who could set her free of her father's commands. She didn't want old Dylan McDoon; she wanted a different Highlander—a very specific Highlander. But alas, the love she dreamed of would not bring harmony to the Highlands. It might even undo the complicated bargains of peace between the rival clans.

She set the brush down and stared at her reflection in the gilded mirror. She had an idea. What if a union between her very self and that handsome archer could tie the clans into a longer-lasting accord? How could she go about devising such a match?

Her door burst open and her mother hurried in. Rhona quickly discerned her mother's current disposition. She'd stood behind her husband, Brian, when he delivered the news to Rhona this morning. She'd been stone-faced and resolute then, but now her mother's eyes were sympathetic. She came up to Rhona and bent down to embrace her.

"Are ye all right, daughter?"

"Nay." Rhona pulled herself out of the hug and scowled. "I shan't marry the ancient McDoon." As if nature agreed, a distant crack of thunder split the air outside.

"Ancient? I'm but two years older. Would ye call me ancient?" She pulled the maid's stool over and sat upon it, which raised her enough to look down on her daughter.

"Ye cannae agree with this, Mother, can ye? Must I marry as Father said? Do I nay have a choice?"

Cait Kilmahew, a woman of wisdom and experience, spoke slowly. "The McDoons and the Kilmahews have long been at odds, ye ken. This alliance will bring an end to the feuding." She put a hand on Rhona's arm. "Generations before us have sought to settle disputes this way, through matrimonial ties. Me own mother married a Cameron against her wishes, but ye remember her, doan ye? She was happy and me father was a good husband to her, may they both rest in peace."

Rhona's face wore an expression of doubt, but her eyes suddenly sparkled with a thought. "Mother, if it's an alliance Father wants, then what about … uh … aren't there bad feelin's toward the McKelveys? A match for me with—"

Her mother cut her off and raised her hand for emphasis. "Nay, old Laird McKelvey's sons have wives and the grandsons are nay yet of age." Raindrops began to splatter outside and the darkening skies put pressure on the room's few lit candles to brighten things as best they could.

"But … there are grandsons, um, I think," she tried to act as if she wasn't sure, "grandsons that doan carry the name McKelvey. Carlyle maybe? Or … Beldorney?"

4

Cait looked off to the side as she searched her memory. "Aye ... I believe ye're right, Rhona. The Laird's daughters birthed sons. I'd forgotten that."

Rhona pulled some hairs from her brush and tried to sound nonchalant. "At the games ... 'twas the archer, methinks, who won and the Laird announced it, proud as a peacock. Do ye remember?"

Cait's eyes narrowed. "Rhona, I'm yer mother. Ye needna try to be shrewd with me. Well do I remember how ye threw yerself toward the lad, elbowin' yerself past the other lasses. Most fortunate ye were that yer father was advisin' yer brothers fer their events and dinnae see ye." She shook her head. "But ...'tis the McDoon yer father picked fer ye and 'tis the McDoon ye'll marry. Sacrifices must be made fer the greater good."

Rhona's eyes filled with tears. "Me heart resists this union," she whispered, her voice trembling with emotion. "I doan ken the future, but I cannae let me heart be silenced. This sacrifice is too great. 'Twill be a life devoid of love and happiness. How can true peace between the clans be achieved if the cost is the surrender of me own peace?"

Cait reached out and took her daughter's hands in hers, her touch comforting yet laden with a sense of resignation. "Life is a mysterious journey, dear one. Sometimes we must face storms to reach calmer waters. I, too, once loved against the tides of convention, but I chose duty over passion. Yer father has been a good husband and protector and watchful father. The desires of youth fade." She looked beyond her daughter and stared out the window, the storm not yet peaking. "Now I hope ye'll find the strength to submit to yer father's will. Ye doan get a choice."

Rhona's eyes brimmed with tears, but she clenched her jaw and worked a plan out in her head. She'd run away. First, she'd feign illness, then she'd order her maid, Mairi, to sleep in her bed and pretend to be her. That might give her the head start she'd need. Since the summer games she had met six times, secretly, with Huey Beldorney, and she was certain he'd whisk her off to England or France where they could live happily ever after. Their next planned meeting wasn't for another three days, so she had time to collect what she'd need to elope.

A flash of lightning was followed quickly by thunder and warned her she'd be struck, too, if her father caught her.

5

***

HUEY WOULD HAVE gone back to Thomas's barn and slept on the hay beside his horse, but Thomas gave him a blanket and sent him to the cabin's small loft to sleep, telling him it was where he and his brothers had stayed and endured many a thunderous night close to the roof, lulled by the rain patters after the thunder passed.

He did sleep well, dreaming of that brown-eyed lass who'd captured his heart in an instant. Awaking early, he continued to daydream, first remembering last summer's quick introduction and then their unexpected encounter in the heathers. She, drawing expertly as she sat upon a summer shawl, a sheet of fine expensive paper on her lap, a sharpened piece of charcoal in her hand, her fingers smudged black, and he, striding through the thicker grasses, bow in hand, arrow nocked and ready should he scare up a grouse on the warm August morn.

They'd startled one another and then laughed as recognition calmed them.

"Fair day, m'lady," he greeted her with a slight bow, attempting to muster a composed demeanor.

Rhona's brown eyes flicked up over him, her cheeks tinged with a soft blush as she returned the salutation. "Good morrow to ye, gallant hunter." Her voice had seemed then, as now when he remembered it, as melodious as a lark's song. "Are ye in pursuit of some winged creature?"

"Aye, a grouse. I've been seeking the telltale rustle of feathers amidst the weeds, but sir grouse has eluded me thus far." He stepped closer and set his bow on the ground to squat near and inspect her drawing.

"'Tis only a sketch … a humble attempt to mirror the grandeur of nature." She looked him in the eyes. "And there be nary a grouse nor any bird in me drawin's, though I believe I could capture its likeness should ye catch one fer me."

He laughed. "Ye want me to catch a bird? Alive?" He glanced around and frowned. "M'lady, are ye out here unescorted?"

"I am nay alone. I've but to call a word and someone will come." She looked over her shoulder. "From there. I sent them out of me sight. And out of me hearin'. Me maid and me father's ghillie accompanied me." She tittered. "They be constantly bickerin'."

"In love, are they?" He sat down completely, his kilt covering past his knees, his socks molded to his muscular calves, a minor bulge at his ankle where a small dagger was hidden. He took off his cap and fingered the feather that protruded there.

Rhona eyed the cap. "Aye, they were wed at the games, but they have little time together, so …" She nodded at the feather. "Is that from a grouse?"

"Nay, 'tis of an eagle, though I am lookin' fer an ostrich every chance I get. To steal a feather and dye it blue."

Rhona cocked her head and frowned.

Huey thought hers the most enchanting frown he'd ever seen. What a captivating lass she was. His heart fluttered unexpectedly. Her beauty charmed him and he was on the verge of saying so when she asked, "Ye're Huey Beldorney, am I right?"

"Aye, at yer service, m'lady. May I call ye Rhona?"

"Ye ken me name?" She blushed more deeply and began to sketch a distant tree.

"Aye. We spoke a brief moment at the games. Someone called ye away and I heard them say Rhona."

She sighed audibly and stopped her drawing. "'Tis Rhona Kilmahew. And the Kilmahews doan mingle with the McKelveys. Or their grandsons."

A moment of shared silence lingered, both souls feeling the allure of the other, yet wary of revealing too much. A warm breeze rustled the feather in the cap and lifted the edges of Rhona's drawing. They stole glances at one another, each unsure of how to proceed.

Huey cleared his throat. "We shall pretend we doan ken the other's clan." She gave a tiny nod and he went on, "Perchance, Rhona, may I join ye in this artistic endeavor? Have ye another parchment? Another bit of charcoal?" A hint of vulnerability made his voice squeak; his heart was torn between duty and desire.

"I'd be honored," she answered, her breath catching.

He took the offered items and made a tentative mark. "Do ye come here often?"

"Aye. Every Thursday, barring rain."

"Thursday shall be me day of art henceforth. And I shall hunt on Wednesdays."

"And what holds yer attention on the other days?" Rhona seemed to relax into an undemanding conversation with him.

7

Huey took a deeper breath and let the easy feeling envelop him as well, as their conversation flowed like a gentle brook. The sun began its slow descent toward the horizon, casting a golden glow upon the landscape. The heather exuded an earthy fragrance, and the birdsong sweetly filled any awkward silences. They expressed their passions and interests with a shared sense of appreciation. He revered the talents she practiced and she spoke earnestly of her admiration for his skills in archery. Yet, they remained restrained by their deep-seated sense of decorum and good manners, as much as they could sitting on the ground, unchaperoned.

Huey felt his heart draw closer to hers and when he tilted his parchment to show what he had drawn, the look on her face—delight, approval—made his chest swell.

A rustle in the grass thirty yards away made him jump to his feet, grab his bow, and nock the arrow. He drew the string back, steady, and watched the field ahead. He could sense Rhona watching and he was grateful she remained silent and still, not asking a million questions as his younger sister, Olivia, might.

The grouse flew up. The arrow met it in the sky and the poor bird dropped to earth like a stone.

Rhona gave a clap and rose. "How did ye see it so fast and make the arrow fly straight to its heart? I am amazed at yer speed and skill."

Her smile was much more the trophy than the bird. He'd take that image home with him in his heart. The bird was but a meal, but her smile was an everlasting feast.

He strode quickly through the grasses to retrieve the bird and turned to see Rhona waving him off. He caught a glance of the tops of two heads, her chaperones, coming up the hill. He disappeared into the woods, smiling, and already counting down the days until he could find her here again.

***

RHONA WOKE TO another dreary day. This was a wet October and not at all the weather conducive to trekking to the kirk. But she'd thought of a solution to one of the obstacles to eloping, that of having a trunk of clothes and items she needed to start married life. The Kilmahews were not known for their generosity, but maybe, just maybe, if she told her father she'd accept the McDoon betrothal without complaint he might allow her to make several donations—skirts and dresses and shifts and bonnets—to the poor box at church. Of course, most of what she'd take she would hide under the last pew and retrieve on Thursday.

Thursday.

How she'd come to love that day. She smiled to herself as she remembered the first time she and Huey had met on the hill. Her nose had itched terribly, but her fingers were black with charcoal dust and she was ever so conscious of not touching her face and leaving smudges.

She hopped out of bed and reached underneath it to pull out several rather nice drawings done by Huey. One for each Thursday that they'd met in secret since that first time. It had been so easy to order her chaperones to stay down the hill and not disturb her. They thought she was an artistic genius to craft such different styles. How shocked they'd be to learn that she'd been in almost the same amorous assignations as they … laughing softly, nudging with elbows and knees and shoulders,

That second meeting had been even more wonderful. Her heart was aflutter like the wings of a hummingbird even before the moment he appeared out of the woods. She had pulled her bonnet off and let her hair cascade in waves upon her shoulders as she paced about, trampling a spot to lay her shawl. Suddenly there he was. She curtsied gracefully and tried not to smile too widely.

"Ah, m'lord Huey, ye came."

"As promised, m'lady. And me heart dances with delight at yer presence." He offered a gallant bow, sweeping his feathered hat off and down and around. They both laughed at their forced formality.

Rhona considered the dashing figure he made in his tartan finery—too fine for hunting. He must have donned his best things to come see her.

He stepped closer. A package of art things lay next to her bonnet and he scooped them up. "Perhaps ye'd be more comfortable upon yon log."

Her eyes followed his gaze and her brows went up at the sight of a perfectly hewn log, made into a serviceable bench. "Was that here last week?"

He held his arm out for her to take and led her toward the bench. "Nay. I thought ye might like it better to be up and out of the way of the ants. I made it fer ye."

She put a hand to the smooth surface and caught sight of another thing lying in front of the bench.

"'Tis jist a simple board fer yer lap … to hold the parchment flat as ye sketch and keep the paper off yer fine gown." He helped her to sit and handed her the board.

Rhona was amazed. "This is … I've only seen wood this smooth on me father's desk."

Huey nodded. "'Tis the back board of me grandfather's desk. He'll nay miss it."

"Yer grandfather? The Laird of Strathnaver?"

"Nay. The other. The Baron. He's abed now and me *seanmhair* fears he'll nay last the winter."

"I'm so sorry."

"'Tis life. Now, what shall we draw today …" his voice lowered to a tender murmur, "… Rhona?"

She handed him a parchment and withdrew from her pocket a large rag. She unrolled it and revealed two paint brushes and three stoppered jars of tempera paint. "I only have the three colors, but I'll teach ye how to blend them … if ye havena learnt."

"I ken little of art or music or fashion. I've grown up on a farm, ye ken."

Her brow puckered the slightest bit. "A farm? I dinnae ken that of ye. Why a farm when there's castle Caladh or Strathnaver or Beldorney Hall?"

Huey chuckled. "Do ye have an unfavorable mind toward us farmers?"

Rhona felt heat rise up her neck. The last thing she wanted to do was insult Huey. "I prize our farmers and hunters and shepherds above all others." In her mind she pictured the lands surrounding Kilmahew Castle. She'd always taken for granted her wealth and station in life. Should she be entertaining romantic thoughts about a farmer? Surely Huey Beldorney, grandson of a Baron and a Laird, was of a station higher than a farmer.

"I'm sure ye do." Huey took her hand and lifted it to his lips, brushed a kiss across her knuckles and set her hand back down on her lap. "But … if I'm to court ye, Mistress Rhona Kilmahew, ye must ken that I cannae offer ye a castle."

"Court me?" The kissed hand found its way to her bosom, where her heart had started to tap a faster rhythm. "Why Master Beldorney, what ye must ken is that me father be a strict man who has chased away every young lad I've ever laid eyes on."

Huey nodded and she heard him gulp as he rose and bowed again. "Fair Rhona, fer ye … I would brave the seas, fight the English, wrestle a wild cat … er … face the mightiest foe. Ye have ensnared me heart." He choked back a tiny laugh.

"Sit down, Huey. I've heard me brothers try out such talk." She laughed freely. "I will assume no distance nor obstacle shall thwart yer devotion, aye?"

Their flirtatious repartee continued on for a fair length of time as they sketched a gnarled tree, a bird in flight, their own shoes, and whatever else took their fancy. Rhona was thoroughly charmed.

"We must part before me watchers come lookin' fer me."

Huey handed her his masterpiece. "'Til Thursday next?"

She nodded and wrapped the paintbrushes and paints.

"I'll watch from the woods now … to see that yer servants come to take ye safely home."

For a single moment Rhona thought—hoped—that Huey might take her in his arms. She'd dreamed of such an affectionate gesture, but it wasn't to be this day. Huey bowed and smiled and strode off to the edge of the pines.

***

THE THURSDAY TRYSTS through September and into October lengthened as each day's daylight hours shortened. On their third meeting they held hands and strolled a bit through the woods, leaving their drawings held down by rocks to secure them from sudden gusts of wind. The following weeks saw a deeper friendship grow between them. They spoke of family and religion and politics, three subjects that might have been difficult, but they eased their opinions out and skirted the most personal comments.

But last Thursday's conversations got quite personal when Huey claimed he could change her father's mind about the McKelvey clan.

"Nay," Rhona shook her head and held her wet paintbrush above the last mark she'd made, "he'd sooner send me off to America to be wife to a savage there than wed me to one of yer clan."

Huey bit his lip. "Och, I dare say that he hasna a leg to stand upon in disparagin' me uncles. But if ye'll let me, I'd like to call upon ye at Kilmahew Castle and present meself as grandson of Baron Beldorney. The name is less prickly than one startin' with an M." He turned slightly on the bench to look her in the eye. "Yer father be kent fer his wagerin' and so I'll wager, too. If he willna agree to me bein' a proper suitor fer his lovely daughter, then I'll make him a wager so outrageous, he'll offer a betrothal to match the value of what I have to offer."

Rhona frowned. "And what could ye have that be so priceless? For priceless am I, ye ken." She added a cockeyed grin to the audacious remark.

"I saw him admirin' somethin' at the Highland games this summer past. Me uncle Keir used the old claymore, the *claidheamh mòr* of me great-grandfather, in the mock battle. I was a wee lad, barely strong enough to lift the thing, when I first laid eyes on such a fearsome sword. Yer father covets it and willna resist the chance to have it."

Rhona's expression returned to one of doubt. "Me father rarely loses when he makes a hefty bet. He tricks a fool with small bets and lets'em win until they cannae resist fallin' fer a more generous wager on somethin' he planned out all along."

"I understand. I've heard the tales and … I've been in situations no one would wager I'd survive."

Rhona left off drawing and stared at him. "Huey, ye must explain to me. What danger have ye overcome on the farmland?" She chuckled. "Did a weed refuse pullin' or a—"

"'Twasn't on me farm. 'Twas at Strathnaver, several years past. Do ye remember the plague what took so many lives?"

"Aye. We closed our gates and turned away all who begged for help that spring."

"Strathnaver was attacked by forty or fifty men of Kincraig and Heathhaven and the surroundin' towns and the clans of McDoon and Ferguson and McNally."

"Attacked?"

"Aye, 'twasn't the May Day celebration we were plannin'. I was sent off, with me father, to track the first wave of angry men who wanted the doctor's daughter. We had a scuffle that ended badly with the death of one of theirs. Then they collected the others I mentioned and came to Strathnaver with stealth and—"

"Wait. Why did these men want the daughter and nay the doctor if it was the time of the plague?"

"She was a helper to the doctor and they'd been accused of witchcraft when they were in Kincraig ahealin' the sick." He stood and began to pace. "'Twas horrible. And I doan mean jist the saddle sores from ridin' between towns, two, three times. First with me pa … and we had that fight against 'em. And then I went with Colin. And he rescued Doctor Muir's daughter, Brooke." He stopped mid-pace to ask, "Do ye ken Colin McKelvey? He married the lass and travels aboot with'em now that he finished his studyin' of medicine and such."

Rhona shook her head, but wondered if the daughter might be the mid-wife his brother's wife spoke of.

"'Tis a long story, indeed, but me point is that I came up against incensed and wrathful Scots and lived to tell ye. Yer father … the worst he can do is say nay to me courtin' ye."

Rhona sighed and looked down. "Sayin' nay isna the worst he could do." She thought a moment more and raised her head. "Mayhaps I can hint at yer worth, but … if I cannae tell him ye're a farmer … I'll say ye're an heir to two fortunes. That be true, aye?"

Huey huffed, but diminished the distance between them in two strides. He pulled her to her feet, the paper and paints falling to the ground. "I must have ye," he whispered hoarsely.

With heart racing and thoughts taking flight, Rhona gave herself over to a most unanticipated kiss. His lips were warm and insistent. His wispy beard soft and tickling. The hat he hadn't removed tipped toward her head and the feather brushed her ear as it fell to land upon the parchments.

His arms encircled her and she moved her hands to his neck, taking in the feel and scent of him. She'd never lived anything quite as exhilarating and briefly wondered if such a tight embrace might result in putting her with child. Her innocence diminished as he pulled back an inch and brushed his lips against her neck and then cheeks and forehead, finishing with another long and passionate kiss that made her lips tingle with desire.

"Huey …" she barely spoke his name as he released her quite suddenly and turned aside. She was panting and so was he. She glanced behind her expecting her chaperones to come racing to her rescue as surely she must have groaned quite loudly.

"I beg yer pardon, Rhona …" His voice trembled.

She plopped back down on the bench and made a squeaking sound.

"Are ye all right? I dinnae hurt ye, did I?" He knelt in front of her. "Ye must ken me strong feelin's fer ye. But I doan have a fortune and though I may be heir to a farm, it willna be enough to interest a Kilmahew."

She let him take her hands and hold them. The warmth of them calmed her and made her focus on his words and not the recent indulgence. "There's been talk between me brothers and me father of clans to the north that they wish to make alliance with and … well, I'm but property to bargain with … and so …"

"Say nary another word. I shall find a fortune … or two … and ask fer yer hand. Would that please ye?"

She answered with a smile.

"I'm off to see a laird and a baron." He grabbed his hat from the ground and swept a farewell bow with it before running to the woods.

Chapter 2

THOMAS EYED HUEY as he came down from the loft. "Did ye sleep or did ye jist lie there and dream of lasses?"

Huey jumped the last rung and landed loudly on the creaking floorboard. "I barely dreamt at all with all the snorin' from yon room." He tried to guffaw like his father or his uncle might. "But it did give me time to think upon yer words of last night."

"Aye? Well, in this land of tartans and kilts and fairies, where love and war dance hand in hand, ye best think on gettin' yerself a bride from—"

"Thomas," Huey cut him off, "ye seem a poetic type. Can ye keep a secret?"

"Mayhaps." He squinted his better eye while the other peered left. "Aye, aye, I can keep a secret."

"I've been keepin' company one afternoon each week with the Kilmahew lass, the daughter of Brian Kilmahew, and nary another soul kens."

Thomas shook his head slowly and brought both eyes into alignment for an instant. "Ye be playin' with fire, lad."

"She's worth the burn, Thomas. I promised her a fortune her father couldna refuse and I've jist been to see me grandfather, Baron Beldor-

15

ney. I'm sure he intends to leave me most of what he has. I'm the oldest of the grandchildren. He once had a falling out with me father ..."

"I ken."

"... and me aunt, me father's sister, has three children yet livin' all younger than me sister, Olivia, so I expect to be his heir ... someday. And Laird McKelvey, me other grandfather, may well have a fortune big enough to divide amongst all his grandchildren. Seventeen there be now. I'll go see him next."

A smirk darkened Thomas's face. "This was once a happy home. Parents had I. And brothers and sisters. But as ye've seen yer whole life ... I live alone. 'Twas a fortune indeed what split me family and left me to tend to sheep and horses. Alone. I consider me fortune to lie in havin' the friendships of yer father and Keir McKelvey and Tavish Paterson ... and ye, o' course."

Huey smiled back. "Thank ye, Thomas, and I do cherish yer friendship and help and shelter. And I agree with ye. I doan need a fortune, but I want the hand of Rhona Kilmahew in marriage. So I need one ... or two. I ... I love her."

Thomas rolled his eyes unevenly and shook his head. "She be forbidden, lad. But do what ye have to do ... and if ye ever need anythin' from me ... I'll do ye right."

Huey waved as he galloped away from Thomas's, his mind already switching back to his favorite memory: kissing Rhona. He'd been bolder than he meant to be and upon reliving the afternoon so many times, he realized he should have strewn more flowery words and been more chivalrous before charging forth with a shameless kiss. Rhona Kilmahew was far above any other lass he'd known and she deserved to be treated with more dignity and patience. It was fortunate that she'd forgiven him immediately—or so he assumed since the kisses were returned. However, he meant to be more patient Thursday next. He was somewhat aware that the flirtatious language of love in some places involved fans or gloves or parasols, but their coquetry had been more open, full of subtleties of word and hints of love, but chiefly an opening of heart and mind to one another. And with their talk of going to her father to ask for her hand, well, he'd had that instant of overwhelming desire and he'd acted upon it.

16

"Sorry, me fine steed," he blurted to his horse as he slowed the beast to a trot. "Me thoughts are runnin' away with us both, I fear." He slowed the animal further to an easy walk. It was a damp but sunny morning and he had a fair way to go. He knew he should be devising a set of rebuttals to the certain objections his father and grandfather would have to the proposals he intended to present, but the bright morn, chirping birds, and fresh rain-washed scents kept turning his thoughts to Rhona.

Ah, the lass was a vision. Her nose still had the pert up-turning of a child's, her brown eyes warm and expressive, her hair like fairy's silk, and her lips … ah, his heart leaped at the thought of their sweet softness.

He'd made her a promise that he'd seek two fortunes and his recent visit to Beldorney Hall had not been without a strong hope of a fine inheritance, as well as the sad reality that his grandfather was nigh unto worshiping the Good Shepherd in person. Now, because of the rain and his short stay with Thomas, he was a day behind in his effort to secure the assurance of a second fortune and to beg the borrowing of the *claidheamh mòr* from Laird McKelvey, his more approachable grandfather.

He was thankful the harvest was completed and his chores with his father had lessened. His sister, Olivia, missed him terribly every time he went away, but he had little in common with a thirteen-year-old lass. The poor thing almost followed after him last Thursday. He twitched at the thought of her witnessing his rendezvous with Rhona.

A strange thought occurred to him: what if a Kilmahew brother courted his sister some day? He pondered his reaction and realized the enormity of the problem before him. He patted his horse's neck and spoke calming words to it that were really intended to soothe his own fears.

"I must speak with me pa, aye? 'Tis a worrisome problem I have if I'm to convince a hostile clan leader to let me wed his daughter. Surely, he'll be more than unreceptive. Me love for Rhona could be considered an act of aggression." He swore with Gaelic words his Uncle Jack had taught him.

***

THE DRUMS OF love and rebellion beat fiercely in the heart of Rhona Kilmahew that evening. Her father and brothers were off to her Uncle Hamish Kilmahew's gaming house, no doubt drunk by now with the sun

17

not yet set. Her mother complained of a headache and left Rhona to sit alone by a smoky fire fueled by wood still damp from the previous evening's storm. It was the perfect time to slip away. The servants took their masters' absences as leave to shirk all duties and have a bit of a respite from their relentless chores and retire to their third-floor cramped but warm spaces.

Under a dimly lit sky, she stole away to the old kirk on the edge of Kilmahew lands, a bundle of her finest clothes clutched tightly in her arms. She knew which corner of the kirk would be the perfect sanctuary for her things and would keep them hidden from prying eyes should Huey determine they need wait a week or more. She thought the most opportune time would be now, before that old McDoon could turn up to claim her.

She reached the kirk and found the doors unbolted, as she expected. She tiptoed into the sacred place and knelt to hide her things under a pew.

"Maiden, what brings ye to this hallowed ground at such an hour? Are ye kneelin' in prayer?"

The voice and presence of the vicar sent a chill down Rhona's spine. She rose, the passel of fine things still in her arms. She held her head high, her determination overshadowing her guilt as she fought not to stutter through her prepared falsehood.

"Nay, reverend, I sought but to bestow these garments upon the needy and destitute."

This vicar was ancient, a stern man of the cloth, known for his piety and unwavering devotion to the poor and downtrodden of which there were plenty under the rule of Brian Kilmahew.

"By hiding said garments?"

Rhona stuttered, "Uh, oh, I thought I dropped one." She hefted the bunch up. "Where be the place ye'd like them kept? Me heart is burdened with the plight of the poor, and I deemed this kirk the right place to leave these humble offerings."

The vicar's eyes narrowed a moment, then a gracious smile replaced his frown. "Ye speak nobly, but a fair maiden of means and none other than the laird's own issue, seems unlikely to be burdened with the plight of the poor. Methinks there be more to this act of generosity than ye let on," he countered, his voice tinged with skepticism.

Rhona thought as quickly as she could. To reveal her real reason was unthinkable, but some tale with similar detail might serve. "Good sir, if ye must ken, the clothes are to be hidden for a lass who plans to run away with her true love. Her … her guardians … uh, they disapprove of the lad … as he is well beneath her station. But there be nary a thing in the Good Book to forbid their union. I beg ye keep this secret. As will I." Her face, though warming from the confrontation, puckered into a plea of mercy.

The vicar scrutinized her further, but the sincerity in her voice seemed to touch a chord within him. His expression softened slightly. "Very well, Mistress Kilmahew. Ye may hide yer, uh, donation. And I shall respect yer wish for anonymity. May yer act of friendship be rewarded." He turned and added over his shoulder, "And a proper donation of apparel, fitting fer those who work yer father's lands, shall be most appreciated. And a few gold coins fer the coffers, if ye please." He disappeared as silently as he'd appeared moments before.

Rhona's heart and breaths slowed and she was more aware of the smell and sound of the empty kirk. Small creatures skittered along the stone floor close to the walls; the faint scent of aged timber and incense lingered in the solemn air. She hadn't been aware of those things, nor the hushed whispers of the rising wind outside or the setting of the sun which now cast multicolored hues through the stained-glass windows. It would soon disappear and she'd have to walk home in the dark.

She hid the things so well it wouldn't matter if she eloped this week or next, no one would find them. Was she being too confident that an elopement was what Huey would agree to? Would it wound his pride not to let him ask for her hand and fight for her? Or wager a fortune for her?

Should she even tell him of her preparations? This suddenly seemed too forward, too brazen. But what was done was done, and what was meant to happen would happen, as the saying went.

She left the silent kirk, and sent a prayer heavenward in reverence and hope.

***

THE BELDORNEY FARM had prospered in the twenty-five years since Hubert and Fenella, Huey's parents, had defied the Laird and Lady McKelvey and the Baron and Baroness Beldorney and chosen a harder life outside the walls of castle or hall. Huey hadn't realized the difference in classes until his teen years, but even then, because of his grandfathers' generosity, he subsequently enjoyed several seasons at the University of Glasgow where he excelled in mathematics and science. He also studied consequentialist thinking, a new philosophy proposed by an earlier professor whose protégés continued to develop this modern attitude.

Huey often thought about his days at university while planting or harvesting or tending sheep or any of the other many chores he willingly did with his father. They were closer now since his mother had passed and they'd taken on her tasks as well, except for the simpler things Olivia could handle.

Morning light pushed him on, bright yet full of shadows. The air was crisp and the fall scents rather nostalgic. When he came to the winding dirt road leading up to his home, he savored the feel of this home-coming, though he'd only been gone two days. Their farmhouse, former-ly a small stone cabin, now rose as proudly as any wealthy landowner's stately mansion to look over the harvested fields. His uncles had helped his father expand the home after Olivia was born. More children were hoped for, but it had only been the two of them and now, without their mother, they really needed to add a servant or two. At least his father had finally hired three farm hands to see to the animals.

He trotted past the row of apple trees, heavy with ripening fruit, their sweet aroma adding to the pull of home and hearth. He glanced off to the right and then left to spot the cows, their bells chiming faintly as they moved. The rhythmic chirping of crickets along the stream behind the home and the distant call of birds were like a symphony of nature that he didn't realize he missed until this moment. It was always good to be home. Perhaps … dare he think it? … perhaps he could bring Rhona here as his wife and …

His heart swelled with sudden emotion as he imagined his cherished home full of life again, with a woman—his own wife and helpmate—humming about the kitchen, the sitting room … the bedroom.

As he rode closer, he spotted the sprawling vegetable garden off to the side. Its neat rows, once full of tomatoes and onions and cabbages, now boasted only the carrots, parsnips, and turnips that could stay in the ground over winter. Olivia needed to finish spreading straw over those rows. Maybe he'd do it for her after he put his mount away. He'd probably find her in the barn. The lass was overly enthused about horses and could ride like a lad.

The sight of the rustic barn beyond the house, filled him with pride and a sense of continuity. He'd labored tirelessly to erect it with his father before he'd gone off to university. The creaking of its wooden doors and the occasional whinny of horses stabled within reminded him of the daily routines that had shaped his life; he was thankful he hadn't been raised in a castle to be spoiled and softened. Though when he thought about it, his uncles, the McKelveys, were the strongest, least mollycoddled men he knew.

He could hear the brook now, its bubbling waters trickling over smooth stones, gurgling and swirling and soothing his soul. He'd bathed more often in that stream than in the barrel his mother and sister used.

Huey dismounted his horse and felt the soft grass under his feet, grounding him further into the embrace of his home. Such serenity. Yes, indeed, he was certain Rhona would love it here as much as he did. Surely, a woman who enjoyed sitting on a bench in the outdoors for a long afternoon wouldn't insist on chamber maids and ladies-in-waiting and a laundress and a seamstress like they had at Castle Caladh or Castle Falaichte or Strathnaver. He had not yet ventured further to see if the Kilmahew castle was as opulent as he had heard; the rumors hinted at gilded ceilings, expansive gardens, towering turrets, and a royal library. A library. A real library. He felt fortunate to own three leather-bound books himself.

Nevertheless, this home was his anchor, sacred in his heart. Like Rhona would be.

"Oh! You're back." Olivia came tripping out of the barn. "The foal won't nurse and father went to summon the farrier. He said old John would ken what to do same as a horse doctor." Olivia wiped a dirty hand across her forehead. Her hair was well-hidden under one of her mother's bonnets. The lass had taken to wearing her mother's things shortly after Fenella passed.

"I'll have a look. I've done a bit o' readin' on the subject." He thought of one of his precious books: *The Gentleman Farmer's Guide to Animal Husbandry.* Huey quickly unsaddled his horse and let it out into a fenced area.

Within the shadows of the stall, the mare, her coat glistening with auburn hues, stood watchful over her foal. The little one was delicate and beautiful; the mare had dropped her this fall, a month past.

"See how skittish she is?" Olivia put a hand out and the foal jerked away. "She's let me touch her since the day she was born. But no' today." The foal's unease was evident. She ducked under her mother's belly, nudged the teat once, but refused to nurse. The protective mare backed further into the stall's corner and touched noses with her young one.

"Ye see, Olivia," Huey murmured, his voice soft with compassion, "jist like us, that wee foal yearns for its mother's comforting touch, her tender guidance. Step back a moment. See?" The mare angled herself and seemed to be trying to coax the foal to nurse.

Olivia's eyes glistened with unshed tears, mirroring the sadness in her brother's soulful gaze. "Aye, Huey, but we ken the worth of a mother's love far more than that animal." She sighed. "I miss her. I do. She cared ..."

"Aye, our mum cared fer us with all her heart. I like to think her spirit is close by, but I believe, accordin' to the Good Book, that she's restin' in the grave, awaitin' the trumpet blast, when all will rise." He cleared his throat. "I heard the miller say his dear wife's spirit would guide him through troubled time. I hadn't the heart to disagree, but I believe 'tis God Himself who'll do the guidin'."

"I miss her greatly. 'Tisn't fair that ye had her all these years and I dinnae have her past me thirteenth birthday."

The mare nickered and the foal made a circle and lay down in the straw.

"Ye miss her sorely, as do I, but we shall carry her memory in our hearts," he put an arm around his sister, "and one day, we'll pass on her wisdom and love to our own bairns. Aye?"

Olivia nodded. "Are ye home fer a while now?"

"Nay. I'm leavin' for Strathnaver. I have need to see our grandfather there. I've a special request to make."

"I ken what it's aboot. I heard ye." She looked at him and hesitated. "'Tis aboot the claymore. I heard ye with yer intended."

Huey stiffened and took his arm off her shoulder. The mare sensed his unease and nudged the foal to stand.

"What mean ye?"

22

"That pretty lass. The one ye meet with after ye ride an hour and then traipse through the woods and enter the heathers."

Huey's brows narrowed. "Olivia ... ye've been followin' me?"

"Well," she turned and watched the foal stumble to its feet, "I went fer a ride at the same time and I wanted to watch ye hunt and ... oof, 'twas a far way, indeed. I needed to rest and so I tied ole Prince to a tree ... and I climbed a different tree at the edge of the wood ... and" she gulped "and so I may have seen ye bein' all proper and ... and ... maybe improper since I saw ye holdin' her in yer arms like Father used to with Mother ... and ye pressed yer face against hers."

Huey pursed his lips. "Do ye ken who she is?"

"Nay."

"Can ye keep a secret?"

Olivia smiled and bobbed her head up and down. "I willna tell Father. Who is she?"

"She's the woman I'm going to wed."

"But her name ... what's her name?"

"Mm, that's another secret. I'll tell ye if ye can keep this secret fer a fair while ... let's say ... keep this secret until after Christmas. Can ye do that?"

She nodded her head as she pointed at the horses. "Oh, look. She's nursin' at last. We won't need the farrier after all."

"Och," Huey grunted, "we'll have to pay him somethin' fer his trouble." He eyed his little sister and added, "Olivia, ye mustna ride so far alone again. Promise me."

Chapter 3

RHONA BARELY SLEPT these final two nights, planning her elopement. And each day she kept out of her parents' way, but listened from around corners or behind doors. When she heard her father tell her mother that the banns would be proclaimed at their parish church the next three Sundays, her heart nearly failed her.

"Aye, Cait," Brian Kilmahew growled, "we'll be rid of the wee thing within the month. I bargained the dowry down and I'll give McDoon the barren ewes in place of gold coin."

"Ye're generous enough, husband. I'm thankful I gave ye sons first." Cait's head turned toward the door and Rhona sprang back, certain she was out of sight, but careful that she presented no shadow to cross the entry. Her mother's voice sounded wistful as she said, "I'll miss her though. She's been a comfort to me after losing the last three bairns."

"Och, I should divorce ye and betroth meself to a younger lass who could spill out more heirs." He laughed gruffly. "But I shallna do it. It be crowded enough with me sons and their brides and me brother, Hamish, still takin' up space here."

"Crowded?" Cait scoffed. Rhona imagined her mother stopping her embroidering to speak. "Our castle has room for all the Kilmahew clan, their servants, and all the peasants what are workin' the lands."

"And they'll be clamberin' for me to take'em in this winter, good laird that I am, since most have lost their homes in wagerin' on last summer's Highland games."

Rhona could picture her mother nodding in agreement. She'd never dare to disagree, but the truth was that Brian Kilmahew would sooner let a Sassenach live here than allow a poor peasant to pass through the great doors.

Rhona listened for more talk of their plans, but the banns were not mentioned again. She sneaked off to her room and gathered a few more things to take with her. She felt it was her right to take the gold coins with her and even the ewes, barren or not, since they were a wedding gift. She knew where to pilfer the gold; her father had many secret hidey-holes, but she'd never had need for money before and she'd left the stashes be. Now, though, she considered taking the dowry coins; she just didn't know how much had been agreed upon.

The thought of marrying Dylan McDoon, a man she did not love, a man with a reputation for abusing his wives, filled her with dread, but not even the burden of societal expectations or the wrath of her father, were enough to lessen the resolution to be with Huey Beldorney. There was an undeniable connection between them. He was kind, compassionate, artistic, and they shared a deep understanding of each other's dreams and aspirations. And he made her feel important. He wanted to be nothing more than a farmer and she respected that. How nice would it be to live a farm wife's life? She pictured leisurely winter evenings with few chores, a servant to serve their meals, and, oh, books! She must gather several she hadn't yet read from what her father called his 'royal library.'

***

HUEY, WATCHFUL THAT his sister did not follow him again, rode at a full gallop until he reached the woods that bordered Kilmahew land. He wound his way through the trees, tied his horse where he usually did, withdrew a heavy sword from its saddle sheath, and walked the remainder of the way, excited to see Rhona again. Waiting a week between each rendezvous was torture and as the days grew colder it would be less likely that they could meet secretly. He'd already considered a warmer, more discreet spot, but they'd have to meet at night and he wasn't sure Rhona could safely sneak away then. All the more reason to present himself to Laird Kilmahew and make his plea. The sooner, the better, but he wanted Rhona's consent first. He would show her the sword and convince her his plan couldn't fail.

His quick trip to Strathnaver had been well-received by Laird McKelvey. The man was lonely. He'd buried two wives and still mourned them both, but the presence of his oldest grandson brightened his day considerably. He generously agreed to give the ancient claymore sword to Huey as an inheritance he could have immediately.

Huey held the *claidheamh mòr* in his right hand and listened for Rhona's approach. Meanwhile he swung the sword about in various warrior lunges and draws, hefting the mighty claymore high over his head, two-handed of course, as he went through several of the moves he'd practiced before the games.

"Och, fair lady, ye've caught me."

"Had I been a knight, I'd've wounded ye thrice already." She laughed gaily as she set her bundle down by the bench.

Huey plunged his sword into the ground and left it quivering in the soil as he strode quickly to her and took her in his arms. Her brown eyes were gleaming, her cheeks rosy, and the scent of rosemary wafted up from her bosom.

"I've missed ye, lass." He refrained from kissing her and studied her face instead, noting the wisps of chestnut hair escaping from her bonnet. "Ye've somethin' on yer mind. I can tell. What is it, Rhona?"

Her eyes filled with tears at once. "'Tis awful. The marriage banns will be published this week. I fear ole McDoon'll come fer me before the three weeks are up … oh … Huey …"

"Shush, shush." He pulled her closer and quieted her with gentle kisses. "I'll pay off the vicar. He willna read the banns this Sunday."

"But, Huey, it willna matter. Me father is keen to be rid of me."

"All the better fer me, I say. He'll nay resist yon treasure." He twisted them both to gaze at the magnificent weapon. "Shall I go now? I'll speak to him at once."

Rhona stepped back out of his arms and motioned to her bundle. "'Tisn't paint and art I brought today, but books and … and gold. We could run away." She kept her eyes focused on the bundle.

26

Huey put a hand on her chin and turned her face up to his. "I'll have ye, Rhona Kilmahew, and with yer father's blessin'. Dinnae fash." He gave her a more ardent kiss and felt her soften into his embrace.

When finally they parted to catch their breaths, she said, "But ... but I have a coat and two dresses squirreled away in the old kirk. And with this gold ... Huey ... we can go anywhere together." She blushed deeply. "If ye mean to wed me, that is. I'm certain the vicar will hear us pledge our troths and sign a document that'll bind us legally. Me father and old McDoon cannae stop us."

"There is nary a thing I'd rather do than take ye off to the nearest kirk and kneel with ye at the altar and make ye mine forever." He took a deep breath. "But did ye mean to run far or stay in Scotland? For certain I am that Laird Kilmahew would search all of Caledonia fer ye and surely he'd come to the Beldorney farm." He gave her a quick kiss. "Darlin' Rhona, let us go now and speak with him. I'll decline yer dowry and make him an offer that, as a bettin' man, he cannae refuse."

She puckered her brows at him. "Now?" A worried peeping sound escaped her throat. "But I'm afraid."

***

RHONA ALARMED HERSELF at her own words. She'd never considered herself afraid of her own father, but she hadn't crossed him in many years. She'd learned as a toddler to be obedient, silent, subservient, and she'd kept her distance from him whenever he was drinking.

She was, indeed, afraid. Afraid that he'd call Huey an impertinent fool, afraid that there'd be a bloody fight, afraid she'd be locked away until McDoon came for her.

"Please. Please, if ye willna take me away, then gather up a support of castle guards and approach me father with a show of force."

She watched his face droop, his smile wither. "But Rhona ... there be no castle guards I can command. Ye've forgotten already ... I'm but a simple farmer. I can offer yield from the harvest, or lambs and chickens, even a fine foal and its mare, but ..."

She turned aside quickly, eyed her bundle, and picked it up. "Gold. Ye can buy me with me father's own treasure." She pressed the bulky sack to his chest. He took hold of it, but set it back down on the ground and put his hands on her shoulders.

"I cannae dishonor me name or darken me conscience by doin' that."

"But 'tis dowry coin. Ye'd have it anyway once we married." They stared a moment into each other's eyes until Rhona looked down. "I'm sorry." She started to weep.

A shout from the hillside path startled them both. Rhona knew immediately that her maid and the ghillie who attended her father on every hunt had discovered them. The ghillie, Donnie Argyll, drew a Highland dirk from his belt and waved it at Huey. "Unhand the lass, ye scoundrel."

In their surprise Rhona pulled away from Huey, but he drew her closer to protect her. It must have looked to the servants that she was struggling against him. The maid, Mairi, began to scream. "Help the mistress, Donnie. Oh, saints alive! 'Tis a highwayman come to deflower the maiden."

"Nay." Rhona succeeded in extracting herself from Huey.

"Nay," Huey repeated. He stepped aside to reveal the sword that he'd sunk into the earth. "I'm Huey Beldorney, here to present yon *claidheamh mòr* to Laird Kilmahew … for a … for a special wager."

Donnie gawked at the superb claymore and let the hand with the dirk drop to a less threatening height. "Och … 'tis magnificent." He raised his weapon again. "But ye were grabbin' at the Laird's sweet daughter."

Rhona waved a hand. "Nay, Donnie. He was helpin' me. I was unbalanced. Tripped meself twice when greetin' him. I ken young Hubert Beldorney. Doan ye remember him from the summer's games?" She looked quickly between her maid and the ghillie and then pressed on with her lie. "We've been friends fer years. Now, let's all—"

"Donnie," the maid whispered hoarsely, "'tisn't right. Ye ken how the laird has kept all the lads away. Grab that sword and let's take him to the laird."

"Ye'll nay touch me sword." Huey stood, hands on his hips, one brow raised.

There was hesitation on Donnie's face and Rhona saw it. She stepped between Donnie and Huey. "Mairi, carry me things fer me. Come along, Master Beldorney. We'll show ye the way to the Kilmahew castle. Let Donnie carry yer heavy claymore … if he can. Then he can go back to the woods fer yer horse." Her hands were shaking and a wave of nausea nearly overtook her. Oh, why couldn't they have just run away through the woods?

***

HUEY WAS ASTOUNDED as they approached Castle Kilmahew. He removed his hat, folded it, and tucked it in his belt, careful to leave the feather free. Then stared unfettered at the ancient fortress. It stood proudly in the afternoon sun. Inside he discovered the towering stone walls were adorned with ornate tapestries. The marble floors were well-polished with few chips. The castle was a fair match to those of the McKelveys. He'd long been led to believe the Kilmahews lived in equal opulence; the rumors were true.

They ignored the laird's valet and the chamberlain, who bowed as Lady Rhona passed. The two servants then gave the ghillie scowls that he'd dared to come inside. Some servants were relegated to the lesser rooms of the castle and Donnie had no business away from the rabbit hutches or the stables.

Huey stopped following Rhona to address Donnie.

"I'll take me claymore."

"Indeed, Donnie," Rhona spoke, her voice shaky, "let Master Beldorney carry the mighty thing now. Then off ye go fer his horse."

"Yes, m'lady." He handed the sword to Huey and backed away, casting a wink and a nod to Mairi once the highborns turned, and an equally spiteful look toward the other servants.

Huey, with a firm grip on the immense sword, followed Rhona once more. As they made their way through the halls, he compared the splendor of the place with his own humble abode. His heart began to pound with apprehension.

Laird Brian Kilmahew was a stern and imposing figure. He sat upon a carved chair so large it seemed better suited to a king—a royal throne, no less. In front of him was a table the length of two shepherd's crooks upon which sat four ivory chess sets. Huey noticed how each set seemed to have been played to a certain point and now awaited an opponent's next move.

Rhona made a stilted introduction. "'Tis Master Beldorney to see ye, Father."

Huey bowed. The tip of the sword made a tinny sound as he balanced it on the stone. "M'lord," Huey said as Rhona took a step back. The lass seemed far more intimidated by her father than Huey was. Immediately he added a further lineage. "As yer daughter said, Laird Kilmahew, I am Hubert Beldorney, grandson of Baron Beldorney and Laird McKelvey."

"McKelvey?" the laird's voice echoed in the room as he spit the syllables out. "What brings ye to me castle uninvited?" He rose to his feet.

"Father—"

"Hush, Rhona. Ye may leave the room. Whatever reason this man has fer intruding here, it doesna concern ye."

Huey gathered his courage and ignored his nerves. "Ah, sir, but it does. I come before ye this day to discuss a matter of utmost importance: the betrothal of yer most charming daughter."

The laird regarded Huey with a hint of suspicion in his eyes. "Aye … she's to be wed to Dylan McDoon. The banns will be read and she'll be united to McDoon before St. Andrew's Day … in November."

"I wish to marry yer daughter," Huey stated boldly, trying to keep his composure, his hand on the hilt of the sword, but by no means in a threatening manner. His eye kept flitting over the chess sets behind the Laird rather than fixing on the disconcerting man himself.

The Laird's expression darkened; he raised a fist. "Me daughter is already spoken fer. Rhona! Leave the room now." She scurried out, but Huey could well hear her gentle sobs beyond the threshold, before the door closed completely.

"Forgive me, Laird Kilmahew, but I can offer more to Rhona than an old man past his prime. A man who has murdered his first two wives, or so the gossips say." He lifted the sword and held it out across his arms as if it were a proffered gift. "Our clans were once aligned and can be again. We can unite our strengths and build an alliance that will benefit both our families."

Brian Kilmahew's gaze pierced through Huey's resolve. "Och, and why should I trust a Beldorney, a grandson of a McKelvey? Why, Baron Beldorney has refused me invitations nigh onto twenty years." He made an obscene gesture with one hand. "And the McKelveys? We are rivals. We have been for generations. Anabel MacLeod was promised to me brother Hamish, but a McKelvey stole her away. Me brother still pines fer her and remains an encumbrance to me."

Huey ignored the statement and took a step forward, presenting the gleaming weapon. "I propose a wager, Laird Kilmahew. Let us settle this with a contest. If I win, I shall have Rhona's hand in marriage, and the *claidheamh mòr* shall be yers to keep as a symbol of our settled peace. But if I lose, I shall leave this castle and never return, and ye may keep the sword as a prize."

The Laird cocked his head. Huey was certain the man was assessing the value of the metal. The prize was Kilmahew's no matter what.

"And what is the contest?" A hint of intrigue flickered in Laird Kilmahew's eyes.

"Perhaps a game of skill and wit? Ye may name it." Huey kept his gaze from returning to the chess sets.

The Laird harrumphed. "Skill and wit, ye say? The male offspring of Laird McKelvey be notorious fer their brute strength, nay their wits." He snorted a laugh. "I choose chess. Do ye ken the game?" He stretched a hand out and indicated the boards on the table. "Me brother plays with me. And me son. O' course me daughter cannae learn the game."

"Fine carved sets they seem to be. I kent the rules of play once. Me *seanathair,* the Baron Beldorney, has a set of ebony and boxwood." He approached the table and carefully set the sword beside two sets.

Laird Kilmahew scoffed. "Wood? Hah. These are exceptional pieces from Norway, carved of walrus ivory."

"Ah, then if ye accept me challenge and wish to use one of these sets … then a single game might settle the question of yer daughter's future … and mine." He watched the Laird nearly drool over the shine of the sword's blade. He added a further inducement. "'Twould be me deepest humiliation to lose and cast shame upon me clan …"

The Laird's pensive demeanor cracked for a moment as a smirk crossed his lips. "Very well, Beldorney. We shall play yer game of chess. Me daughter's hand, should ye win," he put a finger to the sword's hilt, "and a quick retreat should ye lose."

***

RHONA HAD NO idea if Huey knew how to play chess or not. But it didn't matter. He would lose. Her father was obsessed with the game and played on four boards at once. Her Uncle Hamish had only defeated the Laird once or twice. The chamberlain had learned the game and was allowed to make one move each day. Her father always bested him. Her brothers played against her father on any night they didn't go off drinking. They were more equally matched and from the swearing and shouting on certain nights, she was certain her eldest brother won as often as he lost. But her brother was a cheat. Surely, Huey was not.

Oh, this was awful. They should have run away as she had hoped.

"What's the matter, dear?" A friendly, deep voice caused her to stop her weeping and lift her face. It was her father's brother, Hamish, who still lived in the castle; he'd always had a soft spot for Rhona since she was little. He treated her better than her father or her brothers did.

"Oh, Uncle," she burbled, "'tis awful. Me father is playin' chess with Huey Beldorney and win or lose Huey must forfeit his ancestral clay-more." She sniffled. "But if Huey wins … Father will give him me hand in marriage."

Hamish frowned. "But ye're already pledged to McDoon. A deal was struck."

She didn't notice how her uncle's fists clenched at his sides or how his face puckered into a snarl. She answered, her sniveling reduced to tiny hiccups, "Aye, but I … oh Uncle … I ken he's offspring of the clan McKelvey, but—"

"What! A McKelvey? This cannae happen. This Beldorney fellow mustna win." He started for the door and Rhona grabbed his arm.

"Uncle, I dinnae mean that. I'd rather wed him than old McDoon."

Hamish scowled and wrenched her hands from his sleeve. "Get ye to yer room, lass, and stay there. I shall handle this." He pushed her toward the stairs and stood watching her ascend the steps and hurry down the hall.

Rhona glanced back once to see her uncle hesitate at the entryway. She prayed he wouldn't interfere. She made it to her room as directed and crumpled into the chair by the hearth, but after a moment's reflection she remembered she could spy on the men from the butler's pantry that had access to that room. She tiptoed back down the stairs. Her uncle was gone and there were no sounds of a confrontation coming from the room.

***

HUEY SAT ACROSS from Brian Kilmahew and assessed the man's face. There were quite a few gray hairs pickling the red beard and more still on the man's head. His eyes were green and rather close together, his nose wide with flaring nostrils. He made his first chess move and slid the piece lightly across the shiny board. He'd picked the fourth board and claimed the other three were in continuous play with various other opponents. He bragged of his skill then sat back in his throne-like chair and crossed his arms, his eyes darting to the claymore with greedy avarice.

Huey owned no chess set, but there was an onyx set in Beldorney Hall. He'd played against his grandfather, the Baron, ever since he was a wee lad of seven years.

He matched the Laird's move with the proper response. So many times his grandfather had told him to get his pieces out and fight for the center. The chessboard was a battlefield, he'd say, and the pieces were poised for war. Was the Laird a formidable opponent? Mayhaps. Huey would know in a few more moves.

Ten minutes later Huey absorbed the tenseness that had permeated the air. This room, though cold as the stones of the walls, was closing in on him. Between moves he glanced about and marveled at the statues, sculptures, paintings, and vases. Then the Laird would make his move and lock his eyes on Huey in an unyielding stare. He'd have to look away first to study the board.

He furrowed his brow and contemplated his next move. His fingers hovered over a pawn, his bright mind calculating the possibilities ahead. As the seconds ticked away, he caught a whiff of rosemary and heard a scrape coming from an inner wall. Rhona must be near, listening in, no doubt, for surely this castle had as many secret rooms and spyholes as Strathnaver or Caladh. He couldn't fail her. The Laird tapped his fingers rhythmically against the armrest of the great chair as he waited for Huey's move. A blunder could spell disaster. Huey pushed the piece into place. As his finger left the piece, doubt crept into his mind. Was it the right move? Did he expose his position too much? He watched the Laird's reaction keenly.

The Laird's lips curled into a faint, almost imperceptible smile. With deliberate precision, he moved his knight, a subtle shift that threatened Huey's piece. Huey's heart raced as he realized the danger. He had to decide: protect his pawn or seize an opportunity elsewhere. He weighed his options. Time seemed to stand still as he wrestled with the consequences of this next move. With a decisive exhale, he moved his queen, putting the Laird's king in check. His pulse quickened, and a

33

surge of adrenaline coursed through his veins. Now he could see a potential path to victory, a path that demanded he remain unrelenting in his pursuit. Rhona would be his. They could publish the banns with his name instead of McDoon ... or they could elope as she'd hoped ... or perhaps they should be handfasted before the Laird could require some new condition or constraint.

"Och!" the Laird broke the silence. "Ye think ye have me cornered." He rubbed his thumb and forefinger together. Then, with calm exactness, he moved his king to safety, his expression confident, his jaw thrust forward.

With a boom the door opened and Hamish Kilmahew marched in, flanked by two bodyguards.

"Brother! What are ye doin' with a McKelvey in our midst?" He waved his guardsmen forward. "Take that man and bind him."

Huey leaped up from his seat the same moment as the Laird, bumping the board as he did so. Several pieces tumbled over and one black knight fell to the floor, an ominous warning to Huey. He reached for the *claidheamh mòr* that lay across the oak tabletop.

***

In the dimly lit dungeon of Castle Kilmahew, the air hung heavy with dampness, and the cold stone walls absorbed any hint of warmth. Huey was grateful for the single flickering torch which threw eerie shadows on the uneven stones. He stood beside it and assessed his situation. No one knew where he was, though perhaps Olivia would guess at it. Still, it might be days before his father came looking for him. Weeks even.

Annoying drips of water echoed through the chamber, a constant reminder of the fortress's grim nature. There was a small, rough-hewn bench against the far wall, but if it was meant for sleeping on, there was no way his large frame would be comfortable. He traced his fingers along the cracks and crevices beneath the torch and pondered his predicament.

The sound of distant footsteps taunted him, their rhythm punctuated by the creaking of heavy doors elsewhere. His heart raced, hope stirring in his chest as he imagined escape. He cursed himself for offering the heavy claymore to the Laird at the very moment the brother and his guards burst in. It was a silly attempt to prove his innocuousness and show he was not a threat to the Kilmahews. What he should have done was fought.

Curse that Hamish Kilmahew. He'd easily convinced the Laird to place him under arrest for trespassing and even suggested he be tortured.

More steps. Why were servants coming down to this cold place? Retrieving wine? Storing the fall harvest? Meeting lovers? Each passing footfall brought him anticipation and then frustration; these sounds were never for him. Not even to bring him water.

His stomach growled.

The scent of must and decay hung in the air, mingling with the metallic tang of the iron bars of the cell's door. He ran his fingers through his hair. At least he wasn't shackled; he could move about the dungeon, stare up at the sliver of a window that revealed a midnight moon. He paced about until he tired. He'd have to lie upon the cold stones to sleep.

No. He'd try the bench first. He could sleep sitting up, leaning against the wall. He sat down on the hard bench and took inventory of his person. His hat was still tucked in his belt, its feather still straight. He had a bannock in his sporran, half-eaten, but that was something at least. Better to finish it now than to attract a rat with the scent of it. He broke off a piece and chewed.

He felt his ankle. Ah, there was the hidden blade in his stocking, the *sgian dubh* his Uncle Keir had gifted to him years ago. The black dagger had no handy use now, but perhaps he would need it later. He thought of his horse and hoped the ghillie—was it Donnie?—would have unsaddled, fed, and watered it by now.

Of course, his thoughts circled round to Rhona. Her father had ordered her out of the room, speaking to her as if she were a servant. It was a wonder she'd become a cheerful lass having been under the thumb of that tyrant.

He replayed several of their lighthearted conversations in his head. He remembered how he'd told her his visit to Kilmahew lands wouldn't unravel the 'delicate fabric of Highland society.' Well, customs and clan rules certainly hadn't unraveled, had they? He hoped he hadn't put Rhona in a worse position. He wished he knew if she, too, was now locked away.

Then, as if in answer to his unspoken plea, a soft rustling sound reached his ears. He turned his head toward the cell door where a figure cloaked in darkness stood. His heart skipped a beat.

"Rhona?" A whisper of hope surged within him. The human silhouette swayed, shook its hooded head, bent low and let out a shushing sound as whoever it was fumbled to insert a key in the ancient lock. Huey's heart skipped a beat and he rushed to the cell door.

The figure lifted her head, revealing the gentle curve of a feminine face, her eyes gleaming with concern and determination. But it wasn't Rhona. It was her maid, Mairi.

"Is Rhona well?" Huey asked. "Did her father punish her?"

"Aye," the maid responded. "She was ordered confined to her room. The Laird caught her hiding in the butler's pantry and had strong words of warnin' to give her." She wiggled the large key, glanced at Huey, and continued, "He ordered Lady Cait to stay away from her and let her cry whilst he and Master Hamish went off to the gamin' house the Master runs." The key dropped from her hands and she cursed, "Jings! I cannae make it turn."

Huey slipped his hands through the bars. "Let me try."

The touch of Mairi's fingers on his as she transferred the key, though brief, was electric. She helped him blindly push the key's bit and cleft into the lock. It was awkward, but together they pressured the old key to perform its magic. It snapped in half, but not before the tumblers worked and the lock released its prisoner.

"Mairi … where is her room? I will break the door down if I have to."

"No need. She quite convinced me of her love fer ye … with a bag of gold she has. There'll be the four of us escapin' this old castle tonight. Me Donnie is with the Mistress now … saddlin' horses and waitin' on us." She tucked her hand through Huey's arm and tugged. "Come this way. We mustn't disturb the peasants what be sleepin' down here. What the Laird doesna ken, willna do him ill."

Huey understood.

Chapter 4

RHONA STROKED HER mare's face as she shivered. Donnie was saddling Huey's mount and then he'd have to do two more for himself and Mairi. It had been quite costly to convince Mairi to agree to help Huey escape. But now she was willing to see the young couple to the kirk, witness their union, and find a new home for herself and Donnie. Donnie had no idea yet.

It had been a whirlwind of stressful emotions for Rhona this day, first when Mairi and Donnie discovered her in Huey's embrace, then later as she'd tried to introduce Huey to her father, and finally when she'd been caught eavesdropping. Her body had responded with huge rushes of adrenaline. The tension was wearing her thin.

When her father threw open the door to the butler's pantry and found her spying there, he'd been incensed by her boldness. She got a brief look at her uncle's guards hauling Huey out of the room before her father blocked her view and demanded her submission to his will. She was to stay in her room for a week. A week! She'd never been treated so harshly.

The moments alone in her room stretched long as she wondered what was happening to Huey. An interminable two hours later, Mairi brought supper along with the news that the dungeon had a handsome resident. At first it settled Rhona's racing heart to know that Huey was alive, but Mairi had overheard Hamish and the Laird as they left the castle and the conversation the maid repeated made it harder for Rhona to breathe.

She became exceedingly restless, paced her room and asked Mairi to repeat the stunning news again. Mairi did so while straightening Rhona's things. When she dumped out what she expected to be art supplies and instead found the sack full of books and coins, the poor maid gasped.

"M'lady. Why did ye take a fortune to yer hilltop paintin' place?"

Rhona's heart rate spiked again when she saw the look in Mairi's eyes. A daring plan occurred to her. "All of it can be yers, Mairi. Yers and Donnie's, if ye can pilfer the chamberlain's key and sneak Huey to the stables."

"Ye wish to free him?" Mairi's gaze never left the pile of gold. "Do ye love him?"

"Aye, and if what ye heard be true and they plan to throw Huey and his horse over a cliff, then … we must do somethin'."

"But surely yer father will ken 'tis I who helped ye. 'Tisn't enough gold to get to America, fer that is where we'd have to flee to. Or the Laird will hunt us down. Oh, mistress, ye must do it alone."

Rhona strode to the bed and refilled the sack with the coins, then took the jewelry box from her dressing table and emptied its contents into the sack. The books she left scattered on her bed.

"I ken of two other hiding spots where me father keeps silver and gold. I'll fill this bag fer ye. Will that be enough? We'll all leave together. Ye must come with us, ye and Donnie, and be witness to our weddin'.'"

Mairi's eyes gleamed. "Ye'll find Donnie muckin' the stables. I ken where the keys be kept. I'll free the lad."

Now Rhona stood waiting as Donnie readied the fourth horse, finishing by tying the sack to that horse as Rhona had instructed him. He knew neither what was in the sack, nor that he and Mairi were going to accompany them. He hadn't asked questions when Rhona found him resting on a hay bale.

Struggling for a deeper breath, Rhona stayed alert, watching the path for two figures, hoping her father and uncle wouldn't appear first. They'd been known to return before midnight on occasion. Her muscles tensed as each breath became shallower and harder to catch. The anxious thoughts swirling in her head didn't help matters. *Where were they? What was taking Mairi so long to release him?* Her shoulders hunched up and her fists squeezed the ends of the reins.

"Mairi!" Donnie suddenly cried. "What are ye doin' with the intruder?"

"Hush," Mairi responded. "Dinnae the mistress tell ye?"

She went on to speak softly to Donnie, but Rhona didn't heed a word. There was Huey, rushing toward her, scooping her up, smiling in the dark.

"Me love," he whispered into her hair and she found the air to fill her lungs.

"Oh, Huey, are ye all right? Did they whip ye? Are ye wounded?" Her fingers had already dropped the reins and now busied themselves feeling his face and scalp.

"The brutes were no rougher than a tussle with me little sister. I'm fine." He glanced at the horses. "Four? Are ye all comin' with me to me farm?"

The tears came fast and Rhona's words were hard to understand as her throat constricted and lumps formed. Mairi spoke for her. "The Laird intends to kill ye, sir. The mistress here wants to save ye and it'll mean her life—and ours too fer helpin'—unless we get far, far away."

***

Huey insisted that Donnie go first and head toward the sea, many miles to the east. Mairi followed, inexpertly clinging to the saddle, the sack of gold and silver thumping lightly against the horse. Huey rode alongside Rhona, pleased to see she was skilled in handling a horse.

"To the sea?" Rhona whispered to Huey, once they were on a path that wouldn't lead them past any gaming houses or inns.

"Aye," Huey whispered back. "'Tisn't much of a plan, but it came to me when yer maid said yer father means to kill me." He sighed and stopped whispering, but kept his voice quiet. "I was a fool. I wasn't going to beat him at chess, though I was close. Yer uncle exploded through the door as if he already kent there was someone of the McKelvey clan inside. Yer father didn't try to explain our agreement. He allowed me to be imprisoned. 'Twas odd that he let his younger brother take control like that."

From time to time the vast darkness shrouded the moon and stars. The horses slowed of their own accord then. Huey touched the empty sheath on his saddle. "I've lost the *claidheamh mòr* but I'd've given that and more to have ye by me side as ye are. Willin', are ye, to flee with me?"

"'Twas me plan this afternoon, if ye'll remember." She looked at Mairi's back, the clouds passing and allowing enough starlight to ease the journey, then added, "If we'd gone west, I'd've had some clothes to collect from the kirk. I thought we'd go there and, mayhaps, see the vicar."

He smiled at her and he could see her teeth for the instant her lips parted. "Ye mean the vicar could perform the marriage rites? 'Tis a thrillin' thought. But there'll be other kirks along the way." He twisted in his saddle and looked back along the way they'd come. "I thought I heard somethin'. Would there be guards patrollin' the castle grounds what mighta followed after us?"

Rhona leaned forward over her horse's neck and hissed at Donnie, "Ghillie-boy, were the guards aboot this night or were they playin' dice in the attic?"

"Aye, Mistress, they left old Bruce at the front gate and went to the tower room with three jugs o' whiskey. They'll have switched from playin' shakin' in the shallow by now and on to chicken-hazard. Do ye ken it, Master Beldorney?"

Huey shook his head, then answered aloud since the ghillie wasn't looking back at them. "Nay, I've played the more civilized card games at Beldorney Hall, but dice games are a mystery to me."

"Aye, chicken-hazard be a wee bit complicated, but me wife here prefers me sleepin' in the barn when she catches me wagerin' what little we have on bettin' games." He snorted.

Mairi, still clinging tightly to saddle and mane, spoke loudly over her shoulder to her mistress. "Again I thank ye … fer the reward … I freed yer man … and I see the sack here. Won't ye be needin' some of it fer yer own get-away?"

Huey frowned and looked at Rhona who was now bouncing in the saddle. She answered, "Doan worry aboot us. Ye must get yerselves far from me father and start a new life. Ye can get to America, like ye want. I hear the land there be teemin' with pheasants and turkeys and deer and Donnie's skills will keep ye fed."

Huey rattled his sporran and whispered to Rhona, "If we split off from them, I have but a few coins with me. We'll have to sell the horses to pay fer passage to … somewhere nay as far as America." He caught the glint of her teeth again.

She whispered back, "I have me pockets full of me father's coins. More than we'll need. 'Tis me dowry. We can go wherever ye like."

Huey was torn. What he'd like was to take her to his farm. But it only took a moment's reflection to realize the danger that would put his family in.

In the distance an owl hooted and all four horses perked their ears. The path led them down a hill and though the way opened into an expansive field, a fog rolled in and obscured the way. The thick fog was an apt match for Huey's thoughts; he couldn't quite imagine leaving Scotland without a word to his family. He needed to think more on this sudden scheme. He'd faced a few challenges in his life, the worst being the loss of his mother. He'd seen how it had devastated his father and sister, and he himself had been heartbroken. Could he leave them now without so much as a word? He'd have to get a letter to them and explain his sudden departure and warn them of the Kilmahew peril.

He thought upon it as they clip-clopped along, the darkest part of night slowly inching toward dawn. The horses were growing weary and the riders barely spoke now. Donnie had taken Mairi's reins and was leading her horse; the maid continued to appear twitchy in the saddle, but she hadn't complained.

"Water ahead," Donnie raised an arm to toss the reins back to Mairi, "and a deer trail to follow." They had to go single file now, but the horses all livened up, smelling the scent of rotten eggs—a signal that the loch they approached was bordered by decaying vegetation. The men dismounted first and helped the ladies who then sauntered off to find a private spot.

"Do ye ken where we be?" Huey asked the ghillie as they held the reins and tried not to get their feet wet while the horses drank their fill.

Donnie nodded his head. "I've taken the Laird huntin' in all directions. Three days' ride is the farthest. All the way to the sea in this direction. Aye, I ken where we be." He lowered his voice. "I'd be honored to come into service to ye, Master Beldorney. Ye seem a good man. Not like any Kilmahew. The whole clan be full of mischief and evil ways. I heard—" He stopped speaking as Rhona returned, her arm linked in Mairi's.

"Ye heard what?" Rhona prompted. "Ye can speak freely in front of me."

Donnie's eyes flickered between Rhona and Mairi. Mairi gave him an encouraging nod.

"Well, I heard the Laird's younger brother, Hamish Kilmahew, as he spoke to Dylan McDoon last week, by the gate." He bobbed his head slightly at Rhona. "Yer intended, Mistress … but … yer uncle made a deal with him. He wants ye. Made a devilish deal indeed." The sun wasn't up yet, but there was light enough to see that Donnie's eyes held sparkles of embarrassment as he concluded, "Aye, he means to pay the McDoon fer ye and stand in his stead at a secret weddin' ceremony."

Mairi couldn't hold her tongue. "An uncle marryin' his niece? Have ye ever heard of such a thing? Why, it be incest."

Rhona gasped and Huey nodded his head. "I ken of it. In Portugal … and Austria … and certainly in other places."

"Aye, and in the Bible," Rhona said. "I read it, twice, though I cannae remember the names." She turned to Huey. "Me uncle has been kind to me all me life. Perhaps he only means to save me from McDoon."

Huey frowned as a sliver of sunrise struck his face. "Ye'll nay make sense of it, Rhona. I ken the evil of that man. And McDoon, too. 'Tis legend among the McKelveys. This makes me all the more sure we be doin' the right thing in getting' ye out o' the country."

***

RHONA'S HAND FLEW to her chest and she caught herself from gasping again. "To America, ye mean?" Her eyes flashed to her maid and then to the ghillie. Mairi had only been her personal maid for the last year, but she'd known Donnie as long as she could remember. He'd come to their household as a kitchen boy, but graduated to stable hand and then ghillie. A ghillie was the right-hand man of a castle laird. He could read the weather, find the best spots for fishing, track a wounded boar, and hunt with bow or rifle or make a simple trap. She wondered briefly if she'd be safer with him, now that she'd run away. She stared at Donnie as Huey answered.

"Nay … America be too great a journey. 'Twill serve yer maid and ghillie here and give them a measure of anonymity. Yer father willna chase a ship, methinks, unless he believes ye're on it." He paused to pull his and Rhona's horses onto the shore. "Mayhaps we'll send him a

42

missive that says jist that whilst we settle in a closer region. Switzerland might be a secure haven fer us, yet I'd favor France. 'Tis closer and seeking a refuge there might fool the Laird. I assume he dinnae learn the language."

Rhona shook her head. "Nor have I, though me Latin is fair and I'm quick to learn." She assessed Huey's stance. So calm he was, figuring out their lives, ready to make hard decisions, and keep her safe. She abandoned the thought of staying with her maid and the ghillie as quickly as it had crossed her mind. Surely a farmer was as skilled at hunting and providing. She'd seen Huey's skills last summer in the games; he could throw an axe with precision, aim an arrow at a flying bird, lift a caber over his head. Oh, she needn't worry about anything except hiding from her father, her uncle, and McDoon.

"Yer face is pale, Rhona. Are ye well?" He dropped the horses' reins and reached for her. Despite the watchful eyes of the other pair, she let herself sink into his embrace. Mairi hummed a disapproval and Donnie coughed loudly.

Donnie spoke. "Ye can turn north now, stay within the rugged and less accessible regions of our own country. There be ample hidin' places. 'Twould be difficult fer the Laird to track ye down. Especially without me."

Mairi scowled at him. "They must be wed first." She stepped to her horse and tapped the treasure sack. "Mistress, ye must take this gold and get yerselves to America. 'Tis Donnie and meself who can hide in the rugged Highlands." She put a hand to her stomach. "I have a bad feelin' fer meself, that I wouldna make the long sea crossin'. I ... I'm with child, ye see."

Rhona chirped a surprised but happy response. "Oh, 'twas why ye've been sick of late. Ye told me it was the ague, but ..." She glanced at Donnie whose face showed two emotions. He hadn't known this truth and was stunned as well as proud.

Donnie scooped Mairi up in his arms and gave a hoot as he twirled her about. The untethered horses shied back and threatened to bolt. Huey pushed the reins into Rhona's hands and captured the two loose horses before they had a chance to run away.

Soon the horses settled down and the four fugitives continued with smiles and quiet words of congratulations, Huey suggested they sit and

43

rest a bit until the sun was fully up and they could travel on. The ladies agreed; Donnie produced a hook and a bit of fishing line and waded into the loch to catch them a breakfast. Huey had a flint in his sporran and proceeded to build a fire. Then he took the *sgian-dubh* from his ankle and sharpened some sticks to roast the expected fish on.

"Me Donnie'll catch a feast fer us, jist ye wait'n see." Mairi tucked loose hairs back under her cap.

"How far gone are ye?" Rhona asked.

Mairi looked down at her apron front and fiddled with a hanging thread. "Oh, Mistress, I'm most sorry, I am. 'Tis but two months since we wed, but the child will come … early … mid-winter, I'm afraid."

Rhona let a long breath out. She had a question she needed to know the answer to and without her mother to tell her, she hoped it wouldn't be too mortifying to ask the maid.

"So … before yer weddin' night … ye consumated, uh, ye had a … a single night o' passion, I presume."

"Ah, lass, there were many nights, mornin's too, and stolen moments in the stable, the attic, the woods even." Mairi's slight laugh was filled with a mix of embarrassment and immodest pride. "Ye mustna judge me, Mistress, I've asked the good Lord fer forgiveness and so I am forgiven, and we be married now. That sin is as far from me as the east is from the west."

"Ye ken the Psalms."

"Aye, me mum oft quoted what she'd heard. Me greatest wish is to learn to read and see those precious words fer meself."

Rhona nodded. The change in subject made it difficult to ask Mairi her very personal question. She yearned to lie with Huey as his wife, but she was unsure of what that meant. She'd seen the rams mount the ewes and the roosters stand on the hens' backs, but—

Donnie splashed and shouted, "Och aye, what a bonnie catch!"

All heads went up to look. Huey responded, "By God's grace, ye've caught us a grand fish. What a prize."

Mairi rose and clapped her hands. Donnie tossed the fish toward her and she caught it in her skirts. "Blessed be the waters fer this noble catch. Now … three more like it, me husband."

Chapter 5

CAIT BLUBBERED INCOHERENTLY.
Laird Brian Kilmahew was hungover, so ill that he didn't understand the sobbing words of his overly-dramatic wife.

"She's ... she's gone ... been gone all night ... her maid too ... gone ... gone ferever ... oh, me precious daughter ... gone."

The Laird stumbled past the dining chair his wife sat in and hollered toward the servants' hall, demanding his usual morning-after-too-much-ale breakfast of hot buttermilk and corn flour. He set a hand on the table for balance before sliding into his chair. He blew out an exasperated sigh, his breath foul.

"I'll nay abide yer caterwaulin'. What was it ye said? Speak softly and doan screech." He put both hands to his temples.

"Have ye nay heard me? Our Rhona is missin'." She gulped back a sob and looked at her husband from under wet lashes, her face pale, her eyes red.

"Och ... the lass is but off paintin' somewhere. Ye needna fash. I threatened her maid with a beatin' should she let Rhona out of her sight."

"This isna her paintin' day. 'Tis Friday. We pray together on Friday morns. 'Tis our custom. But I found her gone from her room last night and there I slept awaitin'. She nivver returned. I've searched the castle. Mairi is gone as well."

A kitchen maid rushed in with the Laird's cure and set the steaming cup in front of him. She waited a moment for further instructions, but the Laird waved her off with a grunt. He took a sip and coughed.

"Brian? Did ye hear me?" Her voice stronger now, more urgent. "She's run away because ye betrothed her to that McDoon."

The Laird snorted in his cup. "She has another suitor." He took a longer drink, his eyes clearing, his brows rising in thought. "Aye. He brought me the McKelvey *claidheamh mòr* and now 'tis mine. The lad be mine, too, as he's locked in the dungeon." A cruel laugh emphasized the statement. "'Twas Hamish's command. He holds a fierce grudge against the McKelveys, ye ken."

Cait sprang from her chair. "The dungeon? That must be where the child is … to see the archer … the McKelvey grandson what won at the games. She hinted aboot the lad to me." She pushed the chair out of her way and headed toward the door that her brother-in-law now blocked. "Out of me way, Hamish. I must find me daughter."

Hamish didn't move. He wasn't the slightest bit ill from the effects of a night of strong drink. He was, it seemed, overly interested in Rhona's whereabouts. "Is she missin'? Me brother said he confined her to her room."

"She wasna in her room all night. I fear she went to sit with the archer." She tried to push past him, but he put a muscled arm across her path. "Let me pass. I must see to her. She'll have caught her death in the cold dungeon."

Hamish cast a worried look at Brian whose face froze in an expression of pain and disinterest. "Go with her. She'll nay be happy 'til she sees the lass."

"Nor will I," Hamish mumbled. He dropped his arm and followed Cait.

They crossed the damp stones and hurried through the rooms not yet set with fires. They went out the large castle doors and Hamish helped her to the outside entrance to the underground spaces used for storage and imprisonment. Neither of them knew it was also the sleeping quarters of poor peasants who'd already sneaked out and gone to look for day labor.

Cait put a kerchief to her nose immediately upon descending the steps. "Oh, surely she'll have succumbed to the cold and her humours will be out of balance." She slipped on wet stones and Hamish caught her arm. He kept her arm in his as they made their way toward the cell.

"I've nay been down here more than once in all me years at Castle Kilmahew. 'Tis a nasty place." She sniffled and clung more tightly to her brother-in-law.

Hamish stiffened as they came to the torch that flickered by the cell. He let go of Cait and swore, grabbed the cell door, and jiggle out the broken bits of key that fell to the ground next to the looped end of the rest of the key. "He's escaped! And taken me Rho— ... taken Rhona with him." Another curse, worse than the first, caused Cait to back away from Hamish.

***

THE LAIRD'S REACTION to his wife's screaming and his brother's swearing was at first to block his ears. He'd finished his buttermilk, but its effects had not yet completely cleared his fog. But his mind did indeed gain some clarity when Hamish's words implied that the blasted Beldorney lad had taken his only daughter away, no doubt to ravish the lass and ruin her for the McDoon.

Hamish was particularly incensed. "We must gather the clansmen and servants, too. We'll need the ghillie to do the trackin'."

"Oh, the ghillie," Cait exclaimed. "It's his wife what's missin' too." She turned her focus to her husband. "The maid ... Rhona's maid ... she's wed to the ghillie. They've been Rhona's overseers when she leaves the castle. Mayhaps they've already gone lookin' fer her."

Hamish exchanged a knowing look with the Laird. Then he tried to shush Cait. "Calm down, woman. No doubt the Beldorney lad paid the servants to let him out. The ghillie and the maid are long gone by now and in a different direction." He tapped his chin in thought. "They can't've gone far. They'll be on foot, takin' deer paths. The ghillie will cover his tracks, but it should be easy to follow me niece and that knave. We'll find'em." He slapped a hand down in front of the Laird. "Get yerself up, man. Call fer yer sons and go to Strathnaver. I'll send a group to Caladh, another south, and I'll head fer Beldorney Hall."

Cait caught his sleeve to get his attention. "The lad willna take her to those places. He's kin of McKelvey and Beldorney, 'tis true, but there was talk among the womenfolk at the games ... some noticed how handsome a lad he was and the tale was told of how he works his father's farm … a fine lad, he is, still grievin' fer his mother." She bit her lip as if stopping herself from revealing too much. "Ye might have better luck … goin' to the fields that neighbor Beldorney land."

The Laird rose, still unsteady and squinting with head pain. "We'll nay take orders from a woman, Cait. Best ye leave the searchin' to us men." He nodded toward his brother. "Hamish, ye can go wherever ye please. I'll nay stop ye, but I've half a mind to let the lass flounder with the young lad. It'll save me the dowry I promised McDoon."

Hamish put his hands on his hips. "I have me own contract with McDoon and I feel honor-bound to rescue his bride."

The Laird snorted and slumped back into his chair. His wife's sigh was enough to irritate him further. "Cait, get yerself outta me sight."

Hamish snickered softly and preceded Cait out of the room. When she started to beg him again to find her daughter, he smirked and answered, "Dear sister, ye must do yer grievin' fer yer daughter and be done with it. Doan expect to see her again. When I find her, I'll take her to McDoon. Without a dowry, he may keep her or send her off, but 'tis clear me brother willna have her back." He didn't meet her gaze.

"Surely McDoon will have her and she'll be safe. He'll accept her … and her maid … the ghillie too. Why I'm fair certain Mairi willna leave her side." She wrung her hands.

"Aye, but if she's been ruined … well, McDoon can get a price fer her by sendin' her off to England, ye ken."

Cait gasped and then crumpled to the stone floor to weep afresh. Hamish ignored her and strode off.

He hurried to the stables and asked the first stable hand he saw if he knew where the ghillie was.

"Nay, sir, but I jist came from drawin' water and," he shook slightly, "I have to tell the Laird that … oh, sir, mayhaps ye can bear the news … there be three horses missin'."

Hamish furrowed his brow. "Only three?"

"Well, there was that nice one that Donnie—he's the ghillie, ye ken—that Donnie brought to the stable on orders from the Mistress Rhona. But that horse be gone, too. So … four gone." The lad looked down at his feet, waiting for the strike he expected.

Hamish was not surprised. Now he knew for certain that four had left together. It would be easier tracking a group. If Cait was right and the maid would insist on staying with Rhona, then so would the ghillie. He couldn't erase sixteen hoof prints. The trail would be visible, easy for him to follow. Yes, indeed, he'd do this alone. One man with several weapons would be no match for two men who had none. He nearly laughed aloud.

"Saddle me horse. Now." He swatted the stable boy and thought how delicious it would be to 'rescue' his niece.

***

CAIT STOPPED HER bawling and got to her feet. A rush of anger seized her. She clenched her fists and set her jaw. One long breath in and another breath out. Hamish was doing something; her husband was not. Hamish was the brother she should have married, not the one fourteen years her senior. No, that wasn't true, who she should have married was Charles Carlyle. But Charles wed Elsie McKelvey and that was that. Dreams crushed. An arranged marriage was laid out before her. A life she didn't want.

She'd been foolish not to rebel when she was Rhona's age. She could have had a peaceful, lovely life with a gentle man if she'd been brave enough to run away. Like her daughter did now.

She looked around the great hall. A maid came out of the library, curtsied toward her, and scurried on to the next room she was tasked with cleaning.

Cait tensed up again and listened. The dining room produced new voices; one of her sons had entered from the other way and was shouting his breakfast demands. The Laird hushed him.

Both her sons had been sweet lads, but now they'd grown into surly-natured men, so like the Laird.

She hated the Laird.

Curse him! Had she said that aloud? No, she'd merely choked back the invective that so often had been on her lips when she'd had to endure him.

"Lady Kilmahew, is there somethin' I can get ye? Do ye need a cup o' water?"

"Oh … I dinnae hear ye comin' … no … I'm fine … but, can ye bring me me shawl? I … I think I'd like to walk to the kirk."

Cait's demeanor had softened as she spoke to the young servant. She couldn't remember this maid's name though she'd been in service for

49

several months. Perhaps she'd have the girl come with her, talk along the way, learn her name and see if there was anything she could do for her family.

A smirk changed her countenance. More often than she could count she had helped the poor, a secret way to punish her uncharitable husband. Not even Rhona knew.

Rhona! Would she ever see her dear daughter again? Her bottom lip quivered and hot tears formed. She was so sorry now for every harsh word she'd ever spoken to the girl. Rhona was the only bright spot in this dreary existence.

She swiped a finely embroidered lace sleeve at her eyes and blotted the tears. She was never going to see her precious daughter again, she was sure of it. This had been a crushing morning of fear, anger, love, hate, complete exasperation and now resignation. She was suddenly quite exhausted from such emotional turmoil. But a flicker of hope sparked in her thoughts. Once settled into a new life and with the passage of time, Rhona might send her a letter. Might even send for her. She'd have to be ready … with a bit of luck and fairy dust she, too, might escape Laird Brian Kilmahew's grasp.

The young maid came forth with the shawl in her hands. "Grace," the name came to Cait all of a sudden, "will ye tell the Laird ye are accompanyin' me to the kirk this morn? Then get yerself a cloak and meet me in the garden."

She wrapped the shawl across her shoulders and walked to the doors stiffly. The smirk returned. She stopped by the tapestry that hung against the north stone wall. Long ago she'd stitched pockets to the underside, along the bottom, and there she'd hidden coins she'd poached. It hadn't meant she'd run away some day; it had only been a clever game she'd played against the Laird, though of course he knew nothing of it.

There were more hidey-holes about the castle—spaces under wardrobe floorboards, a niche behind a loose stone in the fireplace of a rarely used bed chamber, a hollowed-out space within an old, unassuming book among the Laird's volumes he never read—Cait was clever in her own right. She must collect her little fortune and secure it somewhere else. The kirk was the only place she could think of. There must be places there—pew cushions, floor boards, burial vaults, choir seats, candle sticks. She'd amass the fortune and leave when she had the chance. If she'd ever have the chance.

She ran her hand down the threads of the tapestry as if smoothing wrinkles until she reached the bottom and slipped her fingers under and in. She emptied three pockets and quickly wrapped the coins in her kerchief and held them tightly in her hand. She pulled the massive door open by herself, miffed that there wasn't a butler here to do it for her, but also glad since his absence allowed her to access the small treasure.

Already she was forming the prayers she'd speak once they got to the kirk. Prayers for Rhona's safety, Hamish's failure, her husband's blindness to her scheme, and a special prayer for a chance to collect a fortune and steal away to be with her daughter.

***

HAMISH FOUND THE tracks without problem. Four horses heading east. To the sea. They'd left at night and had to travel slowly. But Hamish could gallop and, with luck, catch them at the ships, for surely they were planning to sail away.

He checked the straps and buckles that held sword, rifle, pistols, and knives, then he gave his horse a shout and a kick. He was off at a run, leaving the path and the tracks and taking the faster, wider road where he wouldn't be slowed by branches or uneven ground. He was taking a chance not following the hoofprints, but Hamish had always thought himself smarter than any one else, thinking ahead, as he did when he played Brian in chess. He'd made the mistake of besting his brother once and never did that again. He could have beaten the Laird in game any time he wanted, but it was a more satisfying challenge to make his moves control the Laird's game and bring the man to an unearned victory each time.

Hamish planned to do the same in regards to Rhona. He'd hardly noticed the lass until she'd reached her womanhood. These last few years he'd hidden his desires.

Memories sifted through his mind: Rhona's innocent smile; catching sight of her with her hair down; seeing her dozing in the library, her face slack yet beautiful in repose; the tinkling tone of her laugh when she'd held a newborn lamb; the way she walked.

He'd give all his fortune for a night with her. But he didn't have to waste the riches he'd hoarded from his gaming endeavors. McDoon had

51

named a price far below what Hamish could have paid. He laughed to himself. The plan was devilish. He knew he'd be damned for giving in to this lust, but he'd made the deal and this Huey Beldorney, grandson of a McKelvey no less, was not going to touch the lass and spoil his virgin.

A few rays of grey sunlight fell like mist along the road. He barely noticed the chill of autumn nor the heat coming off his horse's body. On they went, the road winding through picturesque landscapes he didn't notice, with rolling hills, fields of heather, and dense woodlands. Occasional glimpses of small homesteads in the distance were but blurs to Hamish, though he was quite aware when the road was flanked by stone walls and fences, a long-standing presence in the Highlands.

He slowed to a trot when the road took him through a village, but he disregarded the curious stares and warning shouts and let himself concentrate instead on his horse's hoofbeats and the distant bleats of grazing sheep. The sights and sounds helped him ignore the smells of stagnant water, rotting garbage, and human waste.

It was long past noon, when he gave in to the need for water. It wouldn't do to have his horse collapse under him and leave him without a way to continue on. He heard the stream before he saw it. Gurgling over rocks and pebbles, it was a pleasant brook that looked clear enough for him to drink from as well.

He dismounted and knelt alongside his horse, scooping handfuls of cold water to his mouth. He didn't see or hear a shepherd approach until he stepped into the water with them.

"I've lost a ewe and its lamb. Have ye seen 'em?"

Hamish hid his surprise and eyed the man from head to toe. Too old to give him trouble. Unarmed except for a wooden staff. There was no need for Hamish to reach for one of the weapons strapped to his saddle, though the old man stared too long at the rifle.

"Nay. I've been travelin' the road and seen nary a sheep," he waved a hand toward where he'd come from, "except for a flock roamin' the hills beyond the last village."

They stared each other down for a moment, then Hamish asked, "I'm off to sail the seas. Do ye ken how much further to the docks?"

"An hour's ride, I reckon. If ye're goin' to the wharf at Yarwold and no' the one way off to Edinburgh or Aberdeen."

"Aye, Yarwold, I mean. Have ye been to the sea?"

The shepherd smirked. "Aye, me sheep'll have me runnin' all aboot these parts. Been to America twice, to chase the wee lambs." His laugh was a cackle as he turned away and repeated the question to himself in a lower, scoffing voice: "'Ave I been to the sea?" He looked back at Hamish and asked, "Where be ye from, stranger?"

Hamish led his horse out of the water. "I am Hamish Kilmahew of Kilmahew Castle."

The shepherd's face wrinkled and he started walking away. "Och, I've heard that name." He spit on the ground and poked his staff hard into the soil. "Best ye keep on ridin'."

Hamish mounted his horse and patted the coins in his sporran. He had plenty with him. He could toss the poor shepherd a coin worth more than a lost lamb and its mother, but he was never in a giving mood. He only touched the treasure to remind himself of his superiority.

He coaxed the horse into a trot. He'd gone a fair way when he saw a sheep along the road, last spring's lamb nibbling grasses at its side. What a fine act of charity it would be to scoop up the lamb. The ewe would follow them back and he could return the lost sheep to their master. Yes, a fine act. But not an act he would perform. He had a lady to rescue.

Chapter 6

I CAN SMELL the stink of that fish still on yer skirts, Mairi." Rhona scrunched her nose up.

"Nay, Mistress, 'tis the smell of the wharf. The fisher boats be in now and the noon sun be heatin' up the guts what dried on the pier." She flapped the folds of her skirt anyway to air it out.

Rhona stepped closer to Mairi. The men had left them near the docks at the end of a row of shops while they went to sell the horses. A few carriages trotted past and foot traffic was mild, but it seemed a safe and respectable spot where a lady and her maid might stroll.

The small town boasted a cannery and a saltery on flat land that jutted out from the rugged coastline. Nestled between the craggy cliffs and the bustling harbor, Yarwold was an unusual port. Compact yet straining with growth.

When they'd come into the town, Rhona noticed the change in the October atmosphere first. The air underwent a transformation as a textile factory came into view. Tucked into a cluster of stone buildings, the factory's chimneys puffed smoke that muted the salt-tinged breeze coming from the sea. The rhythmic clatter of looms escaped through open windows. Rhona thought it a rather disturbing sound; she imagined workers chained to the machines.

Next her horse balked at its first steps on the cobblestone streets, but a few gentle words and strokes upon its neck encouraged the beast to continue on. It was a few minutes' walk to the shoreline where the saltery stood as a testament to the port's connection to the sea. Weathered wooden structures lined the quays; fishermen's boats bobbed in the water, their nets draped over weathered posts to dry. The pungent aroma of freshly caught fish mingled with the arresting aromas of the building across the street—a brewery.

A short distance further down and they could hear the clang of metal against metal from the ship-building factory. Positioned purposefully by the harbor's edge, the factory's sprawling assembly yards extended their metallic fingers toward the water, where massive wooden frames stood like giants awaiting their transformation. The freshly sawn timber added its fragrance to the bouquet of Yarwold scents. There looked to be some sort of commotion at the unformed ship's bow, where a group of men surrounded a fallen ladder.

"Mairi, are ye all right? Ye look a wee bit pale."

The maid looked frantically in different directions and upon seeing no other choice, she rushed unto the first boards of the pier and retched into the water. She walked slowly back to a startled Rhona.

"Ye poor thing. Ye really are in a motherly way." Rhona squinted up the street. "I believe I saw a sign for an apothecary. Perhaps we can at least get ye some peppermint tea."

"M'lady, doan mind me. I'll be fine now. We mustn't leave this spot. Me Donnie and yer ... yer young man will expect us to be where they left us."

"Nonsense. Ye're as pale as a lamb's nose 'neath a crescent moon. Come now." She tugged on Mairi, then immediately released her as she caught sight of a weary horseman scanning the docks. There was also a crowd of muscular men running past the horseman and down the pier. They jumped into two separate jolly boats and began to row. A schooner was anchoring just inside the bay and they'd need to bring ashore any passengers or freight before reloading with new cargo and, if Huey could secure passage, them. Between her fascination with the ongoings and the suspicion that the horseman was hunting for her, Rhona hesitated.

She lifted her shawl to drape it over her head, covering her bonnet and shielding the sides of her face, should the man look their way. She hunched as well, trying to appear small and perhaps elderly.

"Come now, Mairi. Let's find that apothecary."

55

Arm in arm they walked past two small businesses and came upon the door with a wrought-iron sign swinging overhead. *Muir & Murray Apothecary.* The door creaked open when Rhona pushed it and a bell tinkled to announce their entrance. She lowered her shawl to her shoulders and preceded Mairi into the shop.

The scent of dried herbs and botanicals was a pleasant change from the briny tang outside. Though dimly lit, the small room seemed to sparkle as the single window allowed enough filtered sunlight to strike the rows of glass bottles and vials and make them glitter. Myriad concoctions lined the shelves, some in jars, some in flasks, some in boxes. A counter crafted from rich mahogany stood at the heart of the shop, where the apothecary herself stood, with a small child on her left hip and a quill in her right hand.

She set the quill next to the parchment she'd been writing on and came around the counter. "May I help ye?" Her smile was friendly. "Doctor Muir is away and me husband, also a doctor, has been called to an accident at the shipyard."

Rhona smiled back and Mairi, out of habit and training, curtsied.

"'Tis me friend, here," Rhona said, "she's feelin' poorly." She lowered her voice though there was no one else to hear and added, "She be in a family way."

"I see." The apothecary jiggled the wee lass on her hip. "I well remember feelin' peely-wally." She set the child down on a quilt in the corner where the little girl instantly picked up a rag doll in one hand and a wooden toy in the other. "I have somethin' better than peppermint fer ye. It'll take but a moment to brew it." She ran her finger along a dust-free shelf and picked a box up, opened it, and withdrew a clump of dried sprigs.

Rhona freed a coin from her kerchief, ready to pay, then as the woman set a kettle to boil, Rhona stepped to the window and looked for the horseman. She jumped back from the window, surprised, when she saw her uncle Hamish ride by. If Donnie hadn't told her what he'd heard, she might have called out to her uncle and begged him to call off the search and allow her the happiness of wedding Huey Beldorney. She'd tell him he'd imprisoned him unjustly. The prejudice against Huey's clan was unwarranted. Oh … there was much she'd like to say … but, of course, she mustn't. She stepped away from the window just as the door opened and a poorly dressed woman entered. She ran her eyes up and down both Rhona and Mairi, then quickly went to the quilt and picked up the child.

She spoke to the apothecary. "I saw yer customers might have to wait." She tickled the child under the chin. "And so I thought I'd come over and see to yer bairn whilst ye worked, Brooke."

"Thank ye, Mary."

The apothecary, Brooke, explained for the sake of her customers, "Mary here is me helper, gatherin' herbs and flowers and berries fer me in their seasons and diggin' up roots now."

"Aye," Mary said proudly, "right out there we planted tumeric. Its roots be good fer ..." she looked to Brooke to finish her sentence.

"Mm-hm, the root is good fer digestive disorders, skin rashes, arthritis, and many other ills includin' the sorrows, er, uh, melancholy." She pointed to an amber-hued glass bottle with a shimmering liquid inside. "'Tis me own tonic to relieve achin' joints, too."

Mary stared openly at Rhona and Mairi. "Are ye the women what that horseman be searchin' fer? He asked me if I'd seen a lady and her maid with two rapscallions." She gave a humorless laugh.

***

HUEY CAME OUT of the shipping company's office, bills of passage in one hand and his feathered hat in the other, and a smile on his face aimed at Donnie who stood laden with several weapons and one heavy sack of valuables.

"'Tis done and dusted," he said to the ghillie. "We have three hours before they'll allow passengers to board. Now we must visit a shop or two, purchase a trunk and fill it with what we'll need for the long journey." He pushed his hat on his head, then relieved Donnie of the sword and pistol, but allowed him to hold on to the rifle and sack. "I'm sure yer wife'll have some suggestions as to what she'll need."

"Aye, but ... sire ... are ye nay forgettin' the most important thing?" Donnie shifted his feet and darted his eyes about. "I heard ye discussin' it with the Lady this morn, whilst I was roastin' the fish. Ye mean to come with us to America, a painful decision for ye both, I'm sure, but ...well ... Mairi has been tendin' to the Mistress fer more than a year and takes her duties mighty seriously." He paused.

"Out with it, man."

57

"Sir, ye need to wed the lass. We passed a fine-lookin' kirk. Mayhaps …"

"Och, I'm nay adverse to the suggestion, Donnie. I ken ye've been safeguardin' the lass on her weekly visits." He cocked his head and raised his brows to infer the actual lack of guarding since Huey had so obviously overcome the security. "I've asked the lass to be me wife … and so it shall be. The ship's captain can do the honors once we're on board."

Now it was Donnie's turn to express surprise. "A captain instead of a man of the cloth? Will God allow it?"

"'Tis but a formality … uh, for convenience. We shall find a proper holy man at our final port. Rest assured."

Donnie nodded absently, his attention diverted by a small crowd at the shipyard. Four men were carrying a man on a litter away from the area and a fifth man, a doctor no doubt, walked beside the injured person. A rider stopped beside them, spoke to the man, and then rode on.

"The devil be damned," Donnie swore. "I recognize the horse … and now the rider. 'Tis that swindlin' brother, Hamish Kilmahew. If he heads this way, we must needs disappear."

Huey chose a different curse before glancing up the road and saying, "The lasses are no' where we left 'em. Perchance they saw him and have found a place to hide."

"And we must, too." Donnie glanced about. "Behind that wall fer now. I'll peek aboot and see when he leaves. And then we best find ye somethin' other than those tartan colors to wear. Some troosers, methinks."

Huey smiled at Donnie's wisdom. The man couldn't be much older than Huey. He had a wiry build, sharp eyes, and possessed a nimble fitness, no doubt born of his skills as a ghillie. He liked him.

"And yer hat," Donnie added, "I see plenty o' caps aboot, but that feather might as well be a flag."

Huey took it off as they scooted behind the shielding wall.

***

THE TRUTH POURED out of Rhona's mouth before she could stop herself, despite her maid tugging on her sleeve.

"'Tis me uncle and oh … I'm sure, I am, that there be an army of me father's guards out searchin' fer me. I'm to marry a man thrice me age,

58

but I love another. But me uncle ... oh, me maid here, her husband ... me father's huntin' guide ... he heard that me uncle—" her eyes darted from the apothecary to her helper to the child who'd become alarmed at the rise in Rhona's tone "—oh ... me words be jumblin' around me tongue. I cannae say it."

Mairi let go of Rhona's sleeve and addressed the women. "Hamish is an evil man. He means to buy her from the man her father betrothed her to and ravish the lass. Now he carries a grudge as black as his heart ... against me mistress's suitor."

The apothecary made sounds of disapproval and gently touched Rhona's shoulder. She reached for two delicate teacups and filled them with her brew. "Here. Ye both have need of this soothin' tea. Drink it slowly ... and follow me." She held a side door open and motioned them through. "Mary, watch Violet and give me warnin' if that man comes here."

Rhona walked into a surprise of a room. A small hearth had a bright fire going; there was a table but no chairs and two rather long divans with folded blankets on each end along with pillows.

"Please," the apothecary said, "have a seat and let yer worries go. Ye can call me Brooke."

"What is this room, Brooke?" Rhona gazed at the bowls, medical instruments, and contraptions on the table, then sat next to Mairi on the first divan.

"'Tis me husband's examinin' room. And me father's bedroom any night he's nay travelin'. The patients sometimes need watchin' and so me father, Doctor Muir, or me husband," her eyes showed pride "oft times sleep on one of these so as to keep an eye on an injury whilst me daughter, Violet, stays upstairs with me. There are awful sights I doan wish her to see."

The ladies nodded and drank their calming teas.

"And can ye tell me yer names?" Brooke smiled.

"This is me maid, Mairi. My name is Rhona Kilmahew."

Brooke's eyes widened. "I've heard the clan name and once healed a poor lad of a deadly wound. A lad what called himself a Kilmahew. The name made me husband, Colin, stiffen. Not in fear, but in anger. I doan ken why."

Rhona sighed. "Our people … the peasants what toil on our land … are abused by me father and his brothers. Overworked and taken advantage of. Me father and me uncle take their moneys and coerce them into bettin' on things what willna win them a penny." She sipped again and her shoulders relaxed. She turned to Mairi. "Are ye feelin' better now?"

"Much, m'lady."

Rhona looked at Brooke. "We'd be much obliged if ye could let us stay a bit … maybe have yer Mary get word to our men that we are here … and safe."

"Of course," Brooke answered quickly. "But … one moment." She went to the window and looked up and down the street. "Ye best go up the stairs to hide. I see me husband comin' with the injured ship builder on a stretcher."

Rhona gulped the last of her tea and she and Mairi set their cups on the table before taking the stairs. Rhona clutched her skirts and hiked them up as she ascended the steep steps. The loud cursing of the men transferring the wounded man to the divan, along with the man's own pained cries, were muted once they reached the top, entered a quaint space, and closed the door behind them.

Rhona immediately went to the window and looked down. Mairi stood by a bookcase and frowned at the collection. She often dusted the many volumes in Laird Kilmahew's library, but none of his books were this large or thick. She pulled one off the shelf and opened it.

"Mistress, ye must see the pictures drawn in this tome."

"Mairi, put that back and come look. Do ye see me uncle? Or Donnie? Or … oh, my … how will we ever get on the ship in time? Look."

Mairi turned the leaf to another page, gasped, and closed it quickly. "Ye mustna fash, m'lady. Yer uncle will move on and if the ship leaves, there'll be another tomorrow." She replaced the book and went to peer out the window. "At least that is what tales be told by the traders what come to Kilmahew. I cannae believe it takes a hundred days to reach America but only a day's sail to reach France. America must be as far away as the moon." She turned back to the bookcase and bent down to examine the items on the lowest shelf: a child's spinner, a ball, and a carved horse.

A shriek from below made them jump. Mairi rose and pulled Rhona away from the window. "Oh, m'lady, they be torturin' the poor man."

"Or mendin' bones. I wonder how long we must hide here. We'll nay be able to leave through the wee hospital."

"'Twill all work out, m'lady. Brooke seems a kind woman. Her magic tea has eased me gut."

***

DONNIE'S ANXIOUS MOVEMENTS and muttered curses grated on Huey's nerves. "Man, will ye nay calm down a bit?"

"I doan mean to disrespect ye, Master Beldorney, but 'tis me wife and me master's daughter what be missin' and any number of improper things mighta happened to 'em. I cannae sit cowerin' here whilst Hamish Kilmahew hunts 'em down. He'll whip me Mairi and steal off with Mistress Rhona and now that we doan have horses, he can ride off with the Mistress and ..." He clenched his jaw and made his conclusion obvious with a crude gesture.

"Aye, Donnie, I understand yer concern—"

"Concern be too weak a word. If that man touches either lass, I'll kill him." He peeked around edge of the wall and pulled back quickly. "He be trottin' up the way we came in."

"Mayhaps he's given up and will move on." Huey took a turn at peeking. "Aye, the way is clear. The lasses musta seen him too. They'll be concealin' themselves in a shop or somewhere Kilmahew would nivver look."

"Like the brewery."

"Aye, ye have a fine mind."

"Trackin' women be far harder than followin' boar tracks or startlin' pheasant outta the heathers."

Huey rose and nodded to Donnie. "Kilmahew is out of sight. Grab that sack and let's find them."

They walked toward the apothecary shop and crossed paths with four men who were just coming out, shaking their heads and proclaiming all sorts of predictions. "He'll be dead afore mornin'," one said. Another added, "Aye, and leave a widow and six bairns." The third swore fiercely and invoked God's name. The fourth said, "Och, the doctor fixed me lad's broken arm. I trust he'll fix ole Dugan."

61

Huey called a greeting to the men and quickly added, "We be lookin' fer two women, a lady and her maid."

The men kept walking but the first man said, "Up the hill and to the right." He chuckled. "But they'll be sleepin' now."

Donnie cursed. "We're nay lookin' fer a hoor, ye mangy seaman." He stepped forward as if to strike one or all of them. Huey pulled him back.

"On with ye, gentlemen. Sorry to disturb ye. We saw ye bring yer mate down on a litter. We thought ye mighta seen our lasses." He pulled his hat out of his shirt and gestured with it as an apology. The men went on and Huey directed Donnie to the establishment beside the apothecary's shop. "Well," he commented, "we're certainly nay goin' to find them in there with the injured man. We'll see in here and then head to the brewery."

***

HAMISH SPOTTED RHONA'S horse among those in the corral behind the blacksmith's shop. He'd taught her to ride himself and on that very horse. Old and gentle it was then; he was faintly surprised that the nag had borne her all this way. He snickered and dismounted, tied his horse to a post that served that purpose, and headed toward the blacksmith's work area. A crude sign announced several other skills of the business's owner, Dunmore McFadden, as well: horse trader, hinge-maker, cooper, and seller of iron pots and kitchen utensils.

Hamish strode up to the open-air workshop. He expected to hear the clang of metal on an anvil and feel the heat of a fiery forge, smell the smoke, and taste coal-dust in the air, but the forge was cold, the air clear, and the silence complete. There was no Dunmore McFadden in sight.

He eyed the heavy hammers and tongs, the collection of horseshoes and gate bars, and the tools hanging from the rafters or strewn about the workbenches.

"Hey-o! Dunmore McFadden! Where be ye?"

As there was no answer, he took an extra moment to peruse the items lying so temptingly in the open. Several blacksmith's knives lay side by side, their blades sharp and their looped handles of varying sizes as if made for bigger and bigger men. He helped himself to one that fit best in his large palm.

He went closer to the corral to assure himself of the horse's identity. It and three others still bore the sweaty imprint of their saddles on their backs. Where was a stable lad to brush the beasts? For a moment his ire was piqued as he remembered how hard he'd beaten a lad that shirked the duty of rubbing down his own horse after a lengthy ride. No matter now, though. He didn't care about these nags, but he was gratified to have found them. No doubt this Beldorney lad was smart enough to rid himself of these animals and use the money to book passage on yon ship. He touched his coin sack and counted the number of coins he had. He had no desire to board the ship, but a coin or two to bribe a rower of a jolly boat and he'd have that rogue Beldorney tossed overboard and Rhona delivered into his hands.

He stomped away from the corral, pleased with his new plan, and with his new acquisition. He tucked the knife into his belt and took note of his growling stomach. He'd go back to the wharf, make a deal with some jock-tar, and find a pub house to wait in … with a tankard of ale, a meat pie, and perhaps a wench to warm his lap.

Chapter 7

A S HUEY AND Donnie passed the apothecary shop, a moving shadow within caught Huey's attention. A man was lifting a small child high and making her laugh. Another woman stood at the counter and a second one was coming out of the door. The woman squinted her eyes at Huey and Donnie, but said nothing, and moved on. Huey glanced up at the sign: *Muir and Murray Apothecary.* That certainly sounded familiar. He remembered Doctor Muir from a few years back when he'd come to help at Strathnaver during the plague and the terrible attack by the men of Kincraig. He shook his head at the memory—he'd ridden with his father to track the Kincraigians and witnessed his father killing a man before the man could kill Huey.

Muir and Murray? It was quite a coincidence if there was another Doctor Muir in these parts, but … something flashed in his head. Could it be? Could Murray be none other than his Aunt Eleanor's adopted brother? But he thought Colin had chosen to continue going by the name of McKelvey.

His curiosity got the better of him and he told Donnie to go on ahead as he looked in the apothecary shop.

He pulled the handle and opened the door.

Huey recognized him immediately. "Colin? Why, saints be, 'tis ye indeed, in the flesh!"

The doctor handed the child to Brooke and clasped Huey's arm in an excited greeting. "Why, 'tis ye, as well, all grown up. I havena seen ye in four years."

The men's excitement was contagious and Brooke and wee Violet added their smiles to the reunion.

"And so ye're a full-fledged doctor now?"

Colin beamed. "Aye, and me wife, too, though we cannae call her doctor. It was hard enough to use the McKelvey name in these parts. We used me birth name, Murray, to ease the tensions. There be a big rivalry amongst the seaman what try fer the caber toss and always lose to a McKelvey. But they accept me now and soon the blacksmith will have a new sign finished. Muir and McKelvey."

"Aye, saints be praised. 'Tis so good to see ye."

"We've been in Edinburgh till I mastered all the surgeries and then … with a little one … we thought it best to plant ourselves here. We live above our simple chemist's shop." He glanced up and so did Huey. "'Tis nay as grand as a castle, but 'tis a good home."

Huey smiled then grew serious. "I'm pleased fer yer success, Colin, I am." He nodded at Brooke and the child. "And I'm happy ye have a fine family, a good wife, and all, but I'm in a bit of a spot of bother." He took a breath and slowly explained the situation—his unchaperoned trysts with a lass he came across as he was hunting, his exchange of the claymore for the lass's hand, his imprisonment, escape, and subsequent plan to flee with her and two servants.

Colin frowned and started to speak, "And so ye've stolen a bride, have ye?"

Huey stuttered a denial.

Brooke chuckled softly. "Ye needna fash, Huey Beldorney. I remember ye well and ken ye wouldna steal a bride. I also ken the woman ye speak of. Close she be and as ye're lookin' fer the lass and the maid, ye needna look further than our own" she pointed to the ceiling "wee home above."

Brooke showed him through the surgery where the ship builder was snoring softly, a half-empty bottle of sleeping potion on the table, and his leg splinted and bandaged. At the stairs Brooke handed the child back to Colin and led Huey up the steps. As they ascended, she spoke over her shoulder to both men, "Seems your Rhona is runnin' away from an uncle named Hamish, her maid said."

"Hamish Kilmahew?" Colin's voice echoed up the narrow staircase. "Ye dinnae say the lass's name afore.

"Aye, she be a Kilmahew and forbidden to consort with a McKelvey, of which, ye ken, I'm family to."

Brooke opened the door at the top of the steps and announced herself. "'Tis only I and ..." she scanned the modest room, her eyes landing on the two ladies sitting quietly next to each other, "someone ye'll be athrilled to see."

Rhona jumped up when she saw Huey enter behind Brooke.

"Are ye all right, lass?" Huey got to her side in two strides.

"I am. Did ye book our passage?"

"Aye." He nodded at Mairi who rose to stand protectively behind Rhona. "Yer husband be next door. We were a wee bit rattled not to find ye where we left ye, but 'twas good ye dinnae stay outside. Hamish—"

"We saw him." Rhona shyly looked at the man holding Violet and asked Brooke, "Is this the doctor? Yer husband?"

Colin took a step forward and bowed only his head as his daughter struggled to climb down from his embrace. He let her go and she toddled to her toys. "'Tis an honor to meet ye, Mistress Kilmahew. I'm Colin Murray McKelvey and though nay a relation to yer intended here, I consider us cousins." He winked at Huey.

"Doctor McKelvey, he is." Huey nodded back.

They spent a few more minutes in polite conversation, all the while Mairi wrung her hands and stared out the window. The moored schooner was easily seen from this upper floor.

When Huey noticed the maid's nervous distress, he said, "Colin, might ye help us somehow to get on the schooner without Hamish's knowledge? I'm thinkin' we need a disguise. Might ye have a suggestion?"

"Please, sir," Mairi finally spoke aloud, "can ye bring Donnie to us? He can follow a driftin' feather to a bird's nest, but he'll nivver track us to this upper floor."

Huey gently laughed. "Aye."

And Colin seconded the thought. "I best check on me patient whilst ye round up yer man. I have an idea how to get ye onto the schooner unseen."

***

THE SUN WAS at its zenith, but hidden by an army of clouds, a convenient veil. A salty ocean breeze wafted through the port, bringing with it the distinct aromas of brackish water, fresh fish, and the stink of tar. Out in the bay the schooner bobbed amid seagulls cawing and diving for the scraps the schooner's untidy ship's cook had tossed overboard. The raucous din was nearly as loud as the birds' human counterparts: a flock of afternoon hagglers were bargaining with the merchants, the seamen, and the shopkeepers along the bustling harbor. Several children ran through the streets or played in the strip of land that the seafarers used to spread nets or knot ropes.

"This will work," Colin assured the four nervous runaways. "I've called in a few favors. Our friend Mary will stay with Violet and me wife and I will don the capes along with ye four. This Hamish will be watching for four people so he'll dismiss six caped dock workers all carryin' supplies to the jolly boats."

He handed out the capes. Once tied around their necks with the hoods over their heads, their identities were hidden and they were protected from the large drops of rain that had begun to splatter on the cobblestones. Brooke handed Mairi a packet of leaves and whispered a brief instruction.

"Come," the young doctor ordered when he heard the sharp whistle, "that's me friend's signal. The diversion is underway."

They crept out of the apothecary shop and were met with mackerel skies, ready to burst.

Down by the wharf Colin's friend was shouting with impressive volume and well-acted excitement about a spectacular 'catch of the day' he'd offer to the highest bidder. People came running to see what it was.

"See it now! Fresh from the sea's belly!" he hollered, creating a spectacle that grabbed the attention of almost everyone, and hopefully the watchful eyes of Hamish, wherever he was.

Colin snaked his way through the crowd, his caped companions also maneuvering through the anxious townspeople, most of whom also wore dark coverings up over their heads. The smell of spoiled fruit and human sweat made Rhona's eyes water, but she kept her head covered and her strides the length of the men's. When they came to the crates, Colin directed her to carry the lightest load, bolts of lace, while the rest struggled to lift baskets of wrinkled apples or stale loaves, and Huey and Donnie together wrestled with a crate of heavy tools.

"Are we bringin' the anchor?" Huey joked, his hood falling back for a moment, and revealing his face.

No one laughed, but they managed to carry or pull their burdens to the end of the dock and lower them onto two jolly boats.

It was then that the hulking form of Hamish Kilmahew rushed forth from the pub house. "Stop that man. 'Tis a thief, a robber, of the worst sort."

Colin signaled his friend again and the man revealed the special catch: a large, wiggly octopus. He threw it toward the dock's entrance and while the women screeched, the men in the crowd scrambled to secure the prize. It was a good toss, the octopus landed with a thud and, still alive, suctioned itself to the dock as a half dozen men blocked Hamish's way and multiple hands grabbed a sucker-bearing arm and pulled. It was chaos as, upon another signal by Colin, a lad emptied a bucket of wet, wriggling eels which brought a pair of angry mariners swearing and further blocking any way to reach the escaping jolly boats.

Hamish was beside himself in anger, certain that he'd seen the Beldorney lad, but confused by the commotion and, not seeing Rhona or her maid or the ghillie, he calmed enough to turn his back on the schooner and the crowd on the pier and stand watch, waiting for their arrival. He'd learned in the pub that the schooner would set sail within the hour. The ship's purser had boasted of having four paying passengers, whom he'd tricked into paying a fare to America, though the ship was only going as far as Spain and then coming back.

He watched a lad retrieve the eels, saw the octopus get divided into eighths, and endured a short spell of rain, barely enough to wet his shoulders. The ship's bell rang. The jolly boats came to shore one last time to drop off a couple of dock workers. Four sailors came out of the pub and rushed up the planks to board the little boats and four other seamen rowed them to the schooner. Hamish scowled. Where were the four passengers? Rhona and that Beldorney fellow must have spotted him, or probably the ghillie had. What a clever lad. Hamish could see the chess-like moves that had been played against him. No doubt the horses were no longer in the blacksmith's corral. They must have spotted him and lured him into thinking they were taking the ship by paying the purser to tell a tale. They were expecting him to board in pursuit of them and then sail away. He would have been trapped at sea for who knew how long. It was the sort of deception he could easily imagine.

But he was smarter than they were. He hadn't gotten on the ship. He glanced out at the sea. The jolly boats were lashed to the schooner's stern, four men climbing the ladder, four more rowers following.

His prey were not on the schooner; he was certain of it.

Hamish ran to his horse, figuring he could easily catch up to them, easily follow the fresh tracks in the wet ground. He headed toward the blacksmith's. He'd find the starting, directional, hoofprints there.

But that wasn't what he found. The four tired horses were receiving a good rub down by a lad and his father, the obvious blacksmith.

"Dunmore McFadden, is it?"

"Aye, what can I do fer ye?"

The blacksmith eyed Hamish, his eye resting on the looped hilt of the fine knife protruding from Hamish's belt.

"I'm lookin' fer me niece and her … companions. They rode here on those horses."

"I paid fer these animals." He narrowed his eyes and stopped brushing Rhona's mare. "Unlike some folks who take what's nay theirs."

Hamish stared blankly for a moment, then he had a thought: "Did ye take these nags in exchange fer fresh mounts? Be they gone? I … need to find me niece. 'Tis important. Do ye ken where she went?"

Dunmore McFadden looked down the hill. He had a nice view of the harbor. The schooner was just sailing out of sight. "Aye, she be on the *Sea Serpent*, goin' to Spain."

"Nay. I woulda seen her board. There were nay passengers."

The blacksmith chuckled and winked at his son. He looked up at Hamish and said, "I'm certain I saw them helpin' load a crate o' me iron tools I sold to the captain. Wearin' black capes and hoods … all four o' them."

The growl that forced its way out of Hamish's throat was pure animal.

Spain.

69

Now he had to find a way to Spain.

Or let the lass go.

***

CAPTAIN MCGURK OF the *Sea Serpent* waddled up to the tight group of four, his weathered face making him look far older than his forty-seven years, his immense girth putting him at risk of being mistaken for a whale should he fall overboard.

Huey had sailed twice before and instantly gave the captain the necessary respect. He bowed deeply and apologized for their tardy boarding, raising his voice to be heard over the caws of the pestering seagulls.

"Allow me to introduce meself. I'm Hubert Beldorney and this be me intended, Mistress Rhona Kilmahew. We hope ye'll do the honors, sir, of marryin' us at sea."

The captain's eyes lingered over Rhona, appraising her openly.

"I saw ye helped with me cargo … hmm …" His fat fingers thumped the buttons on his vest as he considered the request. Behind him, several men scurried about the deck.

"Please, captain," Huey drew Rhona closer to his side, "We paid fer our passage and we're nay lookin' fer anythin' grand, jist a simple ceremony to bind us in the eyes of God."

McGurk lifted a finger to point at the women. "'Tis bad luck, ye ken, havin' a woman aboard, doomin' a ship to sink." He glanced at the sailors that were listening. "But 'tis lucky fer ye that me and me crew doan abide such superstition. Me own wife be sailin' with us this trip." His cheeks puffed up, his smile hidden by too much facial hair. "She'll be glad fer the feminine company and … aye … I'll wed ye afore we leave Scottish waters."

Huey thanked him profusely, introduced Rhona's maid and the ghillie, and bowed deeply again.

McGurk glanced around the deck. "Where be yer trunks?"

"Uh, we had to make haste in our departure …"

The captain let out a howl of delight. "Stole her, did ye?" He smacked Huey on the shoulder. "I congratulate ye, son. But, 'tis a long week till we get to the port in Spain. Ye'll be needin' a change of clothes and it jist so happens that me cargo includes some fine fabrics ye can purchase. Yer new wife and her maid can sew, I presume?" He cackled again, turned abruptly and yelled at his crew. "Stand by to make sail! Lay aloft and loose topgallants! Clear away the jib!" He grabbed at a lad that ran past and twirled him to a standstill. "Robbie, get these four passengers settled below and have the purser see me as soon as we're out beyond the shoals."

The cabin boy's eyes went wide when he saw the ladies, his eyebrows rising so high they looked ready to jump overboard. He shook his arm out of the captain's grasp and straightened his back. "Aye, aye, captain."

Robbie led them down the worn timber staircase, past a beautifully carved door that was varnished to a lustrous sheen and bore the sign 'Captain's quarters.' Beyond it there were three more doors, cleverly camouflaged into the wall. A strong push opened the first and the lad stepped aside.

The tiny cabin was surprisingly well-lit by the single porthole. The walls, ceiling, and floor were fashioned entirely from naval timber, each plank bearing distinctive marks of seasoned wear and superb craftsmanship. It might have boasted prime elegance at one time, but the modest bed with tattered mattress and worn quilt spoke of countless days and nights of careless use. There was a bucket in the corner and a single unlit oil-burning lantern swaying from the ceiling. The ship was moving.

Rhona put a hand out on the wall to steady herself.

"Mistress," Mairi quickly put a hand in her pocket and drew out the remedy Brooke had given her, "here be some peppermint to qualm yer stomach."

"Nay, Mairi, ye'll need it. I'll be fine."

Huey's brows puckered together. "How can the tiltin' and rockin' make ye ill so quickly?"

Rhona didn't answer. "I'll be fine once we're underway."

"Lad," Huey addressed the cabin boy, "can ye fetch the lady some bread and ale?"

The boy hurried off and Huey helped Rhona to the mattress.

"I'll be right back to see to yer comfort." Huey gave her a kiss on the forehead as he eased her down and covered her with the quilt.

Mairi and Donnie took the next cabin and Huey creaked open the door of the third. It was larger and cleaner than the first, had a beautifully ornate mirror with a slate blue frame etched with maritime symbols, a

71

small desk and chair, and a covered chamber pot. The bed looked larger than the one in Rhona's cabin. He decided to bring her here once she'd had something to settle her stomach. If they were married soon, they could share the room this very night.

***

THE *SEA SERPENT* glided smoothly through the water, the creaking of its timbers accompanied by the rhythmic swaying of the ship. In the captain's quarters, the corpulent figure of Captain McGurk sat hunched over a map, tracing the ship's route with a greedy gleam in his eyes. Nearby, his wife, Esmeralda, bustled about the room, her dark Spanish features and exotic clothing a stark contrast to her husband's faded vestments.

Esmeralda hummed a tune under her breath as she rearranged a few trinkets on a shelf, her gaze shifting every so often to the small window that framed the expanse of the open sea.

"Is time? May I go? *Quiero ver a los pasajeros.*"

"Och, fetch me yon cushion, would ye?" the captain's voice was full of authority. She brought him the pillow and tucked it in what little space was left between his neck and the back of the chair. "I suppose ye might see to them now. Have them come here for the ceremony in a quarter of an hour. Can ye do that?" He eyed her, waiting for her reaction.

She was an equally rotund woman, and though smart enough to speak three languages, she was caught off guard by one word. "Ceremony?"

"Aye. I'm to wed a lass and a lad … from two opposing clans, they be."

Esmeralda nearly shrieked. "*Ay, qué emoción.* How exciting. I go now."

She had but to open the door and step out a few feet. The three cabin doors were to her left. She knocked on the first and a weak voice answered, "Yes? Come in."

Esmeralda flitted over to Rhona, her dark eyes softening with concern. "*Pobrecita.* You poor thing. The sea sickness, she is a wretched thing, *sí?*"

Rhona managed a weak smile and a nod, her pale complexion hinting at the misery she was enduring. She moved herself onto one elbow in an attempt to rise and be polite.

"I will bring you some ginger and honey. Oh, I have not said my name. I am the captain's wife, Esmeralda. And your name?"

"Rhona."

Esmeralda hurried to the galley and returned with a cup of tea. "You must sip this. There is more honey and ginger in it than tea." She gave a polite laugh and Rhona sat up to take the cup.

Esmeralda tucked some stray hairs back under Rhona's cap for her and clucked sympathetically. "I used to have this same problem, but I have grown … how you say … 'customed to the waves." She settled herself on a stool and watched Rhona sip.

"The captain says he's to marry you and your young lad … but you do not yet have your sea legs. Perhaps you should wait until … *mañana*."

Rhona's eyelids fluttered. "We must marry soon. I … I nay trust me uncle to let me sail away. He'll learn the names of the ports we'll stop at. He'll gallop till the horse drops and find another to race on … or he'll contract a vessel to follow. He's quite rich." She sighed and took another sip.

"A forbidden love. A chase. *Qué emoción*. There are many such stories where I come from. Passionate tales that wind through history, like ivy on a stone wall. Will you tell me your story? Talking will keep your mind from the churning in your stomach."

Rhona hesitated, her gaze dropping to the cup. "Me father betrothed me to an old man, but then I met Huey Beldorney. Our clans are at odds, but Huey almost convinced me father to …" she sniffled and took another sip "oh … 'twas awful when me uncle came and put Huey in the castle dungeon." Esmeralda's brows twitched at the word castle. Rhona went on, "But me maid got him out and then we escaped together. I love him."

Esmeralda nodded. "I too left all I knew to run away with my beloved." She sighed audibly. "But we were caught before we reached the priest and my father slit his throat."

Rhona nearly choked on the tea.

"*Si,* I cried every day for a year. But that was twenty years ago."

Rhona's face pinked up and she asked, "How did you meet the captain?"

"He was a handsome young sailor. Much thinner then. We both were. I was a passenger on a ship bound from Spain to France. Something bad happened and the ship went down. My parents and sisters perished, but Ian McGurk saved me, pulled me to shore, and cared for me, though at first I could not understand a word he said." She lowered her voice to a whisper. "But love came quickly, as it sometimes does when you are young." She gave Rhona a knowing smile. "Feeling better?"

"I am, thank ye."

"Good. Then let me help you prepare yourself for your wedding. I have a nice dress in my trunk, too small for me now, but I'd be honored to have you wear it tonight."

Chapter 8

HUEY STOOD OUTSIDE Rhona's room and listened to the women talking. He was pleased that the captain's wife had come to see to Rhona. He moved over to the second door and knocked. Donnie pulled it open from inside and Huey could see Mairi sitting upon the bed, looking paler than usual, and chewing furiously.

"I was wonderin' how ye be."

Donnie shook his head. "Me wife isna happy on a ship. We've talked it over and will reimburse ye fer the fare, but the first port we land at will be our final destination, no matter the country."

"'Twill be Spain, the captain said, and I, too, am thinkin' 'tis too far to America. Me lass willna bear the waves of the mighty ocean if she cannae tolerate the gentle ripples of the bay."

Donnie sat beside his wife and took her hand.

Huey cleared his throat. "Will ye witness our pledges? Do ye think ye can stand, Mairi?"

"Aye, sir. I wouldna miss it."

Huey eyed the sack on the floor, its chunky shape curious. "Ye might want to hide that if it holds anythin' ye treasure."

Donnie chewed on his lip. "It did clink a bit as we climbed the ladder. There was a sailor what eyed it a wee bit too long."

Mairi held out her hands palms up. "Look what the rough rope ladder did to me hands. I hope the mistress dinnae bleed. Her hands are more delicate than mine."

"'Tis kind of ye to worry aboot her, but I held her hands. They be fine. The captain's wife is with her now. She's lendin' Rhona a gown fer the weddin'. Seems a generous thing to do."

He turned to go, but Donnie stopped him with a warning. "I doan trust the captain. He seems a dishonest type. So his wife may be underhanded as well."

"What reason do ye have to say such a thing?"

"I read men's eyes. I've learnt a trick or two from the Kilmahew brothers. They be great gamblers and win far more than any man who plays cards or games. The captain has the same greedy eyes. He'll find a way to wager with ye or mayhaps to charge ye more. I'll do as ye say and hide me coins, but ye must do the same."

Huey patted his sporran. "I doan have much left. I expect to have to find work the day we disembark or else we'll starve."

Mairi opened her mouth to speak, then shook her head instead.

"What is it, Mairi?"

"The mistress ... she has her pockets—"

"I ken, Mairi. She told me how she filled her pockets with her father's coins. Her dowry, she said. But I'll nay use them unless I cannae find work."

"Aye ... but Master Beldorney ... ye must guard the dress if the captain's wife is givin' her a new one."

***

ESMERALDA LET HER expression speak for her as she pulled a dress from the trunk and turned toward the captain.

"The lass will look lovely in this, *si?*" She twirled once with the dress held to her bosom. "Are you anxious to know what I learned?"

McGurk raised his eyes and waited.

"The lass mentioned a castle, and a rich uncle, and I heard the clink of gold in her pockets."

Her husband smirked. "Och, the fee fer me services jist went up. A castle ye say?"

"*Sí*. She's a sweet young thing. *Pero muy mareada. Ay*, seasick."

He glanced out the window. "We've barely sailed into open water. 'Tis somethin' else, methinks. If the woman be ill already … " he shook his head "… saints be! She's carryin' a plague. We must set her ashore at once." He rose from his desk and stomped past Esmeralda, whose face lost its shine. He went out the door mumbling about the cost of wharfage fees and harbor dues.

Esmeralda set the dress back in the trunk and cursed herself for speaking up. She'd been happy for all of half an hour to have another woman to talk to and was looking forward to the prospect of female companionship for the length of the voyage. A stream of Spanish invectives spewed from her mouth and she ran after her husband.

She found him at the rail, the wind whipping about his person. She tightened the strings on her bonnet and touched his arm as he was about to yell a command.

"Ian, you misunderstood. The lass is not sick with plague or even dizzy from the motion of *la goleta*, the ship." She pressed her bosom against his side, getting as close as she could to whisper a different suspicion in his ear. The captain reacted and nodded his head.

"Och, nay wonder they ran away." He chuckled. "The lad is a—what do your people call it?—a Don Juan?"

"*Sí, el burlador de Sevilla. Don Juan.*" Esmeralda nodded. "But you have nothing to worry about. I only have the eyes for you, *mi amor.*" She gave a seductive laugh and drew the attention of several crewmen.

McGurk's eyes went hard. "Get down below, wife, and tell the wee sinners I'll nay perform the ceremony until the morrow."

"*Mañana*? But why?" She stepped back and grabbed the rail as the ship crested a particularly high wave.

"Look. 'Tis unusual to have such seas this late in the day. I fear we'll be doin' battle with the wind and waves 'til long after the sun sets." He glanced around the deck and saw the other man who'd come on board with the eloping couple. He waved him over.

Donnie held his arms out for balance and staggered like a drunk as the ship rolled. He made it to the captain and bowed as well as he could. "Do ye have need of me, captain?"

"I suspect there be a woman on board that be in a family way?"

Donnie made a face that signaled agreement. "The bairn willna come fer several months, if ye're thinkin' there be bad luck to come of it."

"Nay. 'Tis good luck for a babe to be born at sea." He glanced at Esmeralda who looked down at the deck floorboards spackled with sea water. "Off with ye, woman." To Donnie he said, "Tell yer master that we're comin' into bad weather and ye all must stay below until the morn. There'll be nay weddin' tonight."

***

"WHY, YE'RE BURNIN'" up with the fever!" Mairi bent over Rhona, one hand braced on the bed's side board and the other on Rhona's forehead. "What was it the captain's wife made ye drink?"

"Tea … with honey … and, and … ginger."

The cup rolled out from under the bed as the ship tipped starboard and Mairi grabbed it. She sniffed the cup and tipped it up and over her mouth to let the last drop land on her tongue.

"Sweet," was all she said before patting Rhona's arm and saying, "I'll be back with some cool water and cloths fer yer head."

"Wait," Rhona flung an arm out to stop her, "I doan want Huey to see me like this."

"Ye needna fash, m'lady. I'll have me Donnie guard the door and I'll tell the lad meself that ye're nay up to marryin' him jist yet." Mairi puckered her lips and stared a moment longer at the lass. "'Tisn't the time of yer courses, is it?"

Rhona rolled her head side to side. "Nay, 'tis an evil spirit fer sure what's poundin' a dozen hammers in me head." She groaned and rolled to her other side.

Mairi shook her head helplessly and left the tiny room, pulling the door closed behind herself. She immediately came face to face with the captain's wife who raised a ragged kerchief to her face and covered her mouth and nose.

"Ma'am," Mairi whispered, "mi mistress be sufferin'. The weddin' must be postponed."

Esmeralda nodded. "The captain has already made that decision. The sea is angry." Donnie came up behind her and she raised a dark eyebrow at him, but kept the kerchief in place. "And you're all expected to stay in your cabins till the waves become … *sometidas* … flat." The third door opened and Huey looked out. "Did you hear, *señor*? You must all stay in your cabins tonight."

Donnie nodded at Huey. "Aye, sir, the captain's orders. Ye'll nay have yer weddin'." A particularly bad wave tossed them all against the wall.

Donnie helped his wife regain her balance and Huey lent a hand to Esmeralda who still kept a tight cover over her nose. "*Gracias, señor.*"

"Is Rhona all right?"

"Ye cannae see her, sir. Her wishes."

"And the captain's," Esmeralda said. "She has the plague, he fears, but I think I have convinced him she is ... how you say? ... embarrassed? ... or ... with child?"

Mairi's hand went to her stomach. "Nay, the mistress is a virgin. 'Tis I who ..." she grabbed at Donnie's hand "... we will have a child. He be me husband."

Esmeralda's brow quirked into a frown. She kept the kerchief in place.

"Ma'am," Mairi cocked her head, "'tis the plague ye fear and that's what's keeping ye from breathin' our air, aye? Ye needna fash so. 'Tis only the vapors or some such ordinary thing. Me mistress be sufferin' with a fever though. I was comin' to ask ye fer water and cloths to cool her brow."

"A fever? So soon?" Under her breath and muted by the kerchief, she mumbled, "Ian was right. It must be the plague." She backed away further and ordered them, "To your rooms, and stay there if you do not want to be thrown overboard. We will anchor somewhere in the morning and you'll all be made to go ashore. You must make *cuarentena*."

"Quarantine?" Huey looked hard at the woman.

"*Sí.*" With that she hurried to the nearest door, that of the captain's cabin, and rushed inside. She left the door open a crack and spoke again, the kerchief now gone. She scowled at the three and insisted, "Go. Get inside. Now." Mairi and Donnie almost fell through their door as they opened it when the ship lurched. Huey glared back at Esmeralda before turning to his door and opening it.

But as soon as Esmeralda slammed her door, Huey spun around and pushed open the door to Rhona's small cabin.

"Rhona?" He knelt by the bed and touched her shoulder, pulled her toward him, and put his fingers on her cheek. "Saints be! Ye're burnin' up." He scooped her into his arms and she clung to his neck, mumbling.

Between the schooner's heaving and pitching, he managed to carry her to his larger room. But once he laid her down, a mighty roll sent him to the floor.

***

ESMERALDA HESITATED TO light the oil lamp in the cabin, the one that swung from the ceiling and was less than half full. Fire aboard a ship was dangerous, but she hated the dark. The captain was up top and would stay there until the storm passed or morning came. She decided the risk wasn't worth it and she'd be better off strapped into the hammock her husband had made for her to use during rough weather. She didn't need light if she was going to have her eyes closed anyway. Closed tightly and praying the illness aboard was not a plague.

Chapter 9

HUEY HAD NO idea what to do for Rhona. He held her hand and prayed. Then he whispered promises and hopes in her ear and kissed her fingers. She made tiny groans from time to time. He was at his wit's end and knew he had to do something, but what? It came to his heart as quietly as an answered prayer: he opened the small porthole and held the edge of a quilt up to the opening. With the next roll of the ship, water splashed onto the fabric and soaked it. He closed the porthole and pressed the cool, wet cloth to her forehead. He tended her as well as he could.

The storm outside was unrelenting. He had no idea the sea could have such fury. He could sense the lightning that tore across the sky from slivers of light around the porthole, then it clapped its thunder close enough to make him jump and fear that the ship might be struck.

And then it was. He felt it. Knew it by God's whispered warning in his heart and by the shouts of crewmen. His heart pounded with indecision. Would there be an uncontrollable fire or would the lashing rain snuff it out? Should they stay in the cabin or should he carry Rhona out and get Donnie to help him?

"Abandon ship!" came the call. He heard Mairi's screams and then his door was shoved open.

"Oh, thank the Good Lord," Mairi gasped, "she be with ye. Come. Donnie, help him. We must do as the captain says. Those of us who cannae swim will be rowed away in the jolly boats. Can ye swim, Master Beldorney?"

Huey nodded and gathered Rhona up, thinking back to the time his uncle Keir had taught him to swim at Castle Caladh. Again he silently prayed, this time that he'd have the strength to keep Rhona's head above water.

Donnie held the door and Huey slipped through, surprised by the bright yellow flames devouring the ship despite the heavy downpour. He caught a glimpse of Esmeralda, her arms full of possessions that would undoubtedly soon be at the bottom of the sea. He noticed Donnie's sack, the man's grip on it as tight as his own on the lass in his arms.

They went out onto the deck where rain whipped through the air and slashed them, seemingly from all directions. The deck was slippery and he battled to keep his footing amid the rocking and rolling. He scrunched Rhona up closer and sheltered her face with his neck and chin, her heat not abating. Crewmen were tossing things that floated overboard and plunging into the sea after them. He could hear the captain yelling for the anchor to be dropped and he briefly wondered why.

There was an inferno behind them now; the lightning had struck the mast and run down the pole. Smoke choked the air. He knew the jolly boats were at the stern, but the fire prohibited their passage. They'd have to go overboard as the others were doing.

"Stay with me," he yelled to Mairi and Donnie. "Ye can swim, aye?" Both shook their heads. "Then grab one of those barrels together and hold it as ye jump." Another lightning bolt brightened the sky for a moment and Huey hoped the outline he saw was indeed land, close enough to get to.

He watched the maid and ghillie clasp hands and jump with the barrel. He wasn't sure what to do for himself and Rhona. Then he saw a length of rope, untethered, one end frayed or perhaps burned. He set Rhona down on the deck. Her head lolled to one side. He grabbed the rope while more crew lurched and lunged around him. There was not a barrel left by the time he got the rope tied around Rhona and lashed to himself.

"Stay with me, me love," he murmured, his voice trembling as he eased her over the railing. With the fire licking at his heels, the weight of her pulling the rope tighter, and a distant crack of thunder, he got both legs over and they fell straight down as the ship listed to starboard.

It was a shock to hit the water. Rhona snapped back to consciousness. She gasped and clawed at the waves, her fevered eyes wide with terror. He shouted words of reassurance, but they were quickly swallowed by the roar of the storm and the wash of the waves. He sputtered and choked and treaded water with all his might. The sea raged around them, the waves monstrous and unforgiving. He swallowed a mouthful of salty spray. His arms ached as he struggled to keep himself and Rhona afloat amidst the churning waters. The weight of Rhona's gold-filled pockets threatened to drag them beneath the surface, but he refused to let it happen. A broken piece of the ship's debris bumped him hard in the back and he threw an arm over it.

From the barrels tossing nearby he heard shouted prayers and gagging curses.

"Can ye put an arm across?" he begged Rhona. She, wide awake and shivering fiercely, threw both arms over the wooden plank. Huey instantly felt relief; the strain of swimming for two was eased and had it been a sunny afternoon, it might have been a pleasant kick-about in a pond, but as it was they were still in imminent danger of drowning, being sucked down by the vortex around the sinking ship, or smashed by floating cargo crates.

A long and dark hour passed in which the storm showed no mercy. The cries for help slowly faded into the distance as the crewmen either succumbed to exhaustion or found their way to shore. Huey hoped it was the latter.

As dawn's faint light began to break through the retreating clouds, the sea at last relented, the waves calmed, and hope surged. Fatigue had not claimed Huey's limbs. With steady determination, he began to kick and paddle them toward the silhouette of land.

As the first full light of dawn bathed the shore ahead in a soft glow, Huey nudged Rhona. Her head lay on her arm and his tapping on her elbow startled her. She came alive and kicked and splashed about, letting go of the plank and almost sinking. The rope that lashed them together held her at his side and she grabbed at the wood again.

"We survived," she said, spitting and crying and laughing all at once.

"Aye, we survived." His feet touched ground and soon they were walking in shallower water. The beach ahead was strewn with debris, but devoid of survivors. It was only them.

"Oh, what shall we do?" Rhona's voice cracked. "Mairi? Donnie! Where are ye?"

Huey stumbled and almost pulled Rhona down with him. He caught himself and quickly untied them.

"Are ye all right, lass?" He put a wet hand to her forehead. "The fever has left ye. 'Twas the cold sea what cured ye."

She burrowed into his embrace. "What do we do now?"

***

RHONA NOTICED HOW long their shadows were across the deserted shore. That must mean something about where they were, but she knew little of geography and though she'd avidly read many of the books in her father's horded library, she'd left the tomes of maps unopened.

She was drenched, shivering, and numb. She struggled to wring the saltwater from her clothes, her eyes darting about for signs of her maid. The thought that Mairi might still be in the water, or worse, at the bottom of the sea, was almost too much to bear.

Huey spoke softly. "I'll leave ye fer but a moment to follow yon trail. Mayhaps yer maid and her man are jist beyond our sight. Will ye be all right alone for a wee bit? Ye need to rest."

She touched his hand. "Ye tied me to yerself. Ye saved me. Thank ye."

He pulled her close and caressed her. Gently he whispered, "With nay holy man to wed us, nor the captain able, and as we dinnae tie cords around our wrists and make our own promises in a hand-fastin' rite, I claim ye as me wife anyway. We were knotted together with the sea ropes, we were. Do ye accept me as yer husband?"

"I do."

The shivers left her and were replaced by Huey's warmth. Though sodden, their bodies pressed together tightly and they shared a kiss that neither wanted to end.

"'Twill only be minutes. I willna go beyond yer call." He turned and slogged across the beach and disappeared into the underbrush, then beyond the trees.

84

Alone, Rhona peeled off her soaked garments, her skin prickling from the salt. There was the chance a sailor, one or more, might come upon her, but she could not dwell on that vulnerability, though her eyes darted about, continually confirming that she was, indeed, alone.

She draped the wet things over low branches to dry, her fingers trembling as she worked, squeezing, wringing, stretching. Save for the gentle lap of waves and the occasional cry of a seabird, the silence was deafening. She felt exposed, her modesty stripped away by necessity. She stood facing the gentle morning breeze in nothing but a sheer undergarment, a chemise that would dry on her body before the other things on the branches.

She heard Huey's call from afar much sooner than she expected. Suddenly feeling shy and improper, she glanced around for a place to hide herself, then thought better of it and remained boldly indecent, though most of her skin was covered.

"Did ye find anythin' … husband?" she asked, her voice coming out stilted.

"Aye, wife, I did. There were signs of a camp not far, a type of bothan, methinks, though I cannae say fer sure if we be in France or England or still in Scotland." He held out a hand and showed her a bit of flint he'd taken from the shelter. "I'll collect some of this driftwood and make us a fire here. Later we can go to the shelter fer the night."

She helped him pile the wood then sat on the ground and watched him bring a fire to life.

"What happened?" she asked. "I doan remember anything before finding meself flailin' in the sea and seein' the ship aflame."

"We were struck by lighnin'. The captain called to abandon ship." He cast a look out toward the sea. The sun sparkled on the waters, all the menace of the night before but a memory.

Their conversation focused on the weight of their situation. Huey repeatedly asked her how she felt and she truthfully answered that the fever, the headaches, and the nausea had all evaporated. They listened hard for human voices, scanned the beach and the water often, and speculated on whether this was an island or not.

"Ye must dry yer things, as well, Huey. As yer … wife … I will tend to them, dry them next to mine." She gave him a shy smile.

He shook his head and found a couple sticks. He perched his boots on the ends of each and roasted them over the coals. "I'll dry me boots and then yer shoes. Me wet clothes willna bother me. They will dry as quickly on me shoulders as they would on a limb." He patted a stocking. "I have me dagger. Me sporran still holds a coin or two. I do lament the loss of me hat though." He attempted to groom his tangled hair with his fingers and Rhona did the same with her long tresses.

It was well after noon when Rhona pronounced her dress dry enough to don. She hesitated. "Unless ye wish to … wish to exert yer husbandly rights o'er me." She didn't meet his eyes.

Huey stepped to her side and said, "Aye, I wish to, but we shall wait. May I help ye with the gown?" He touched one of the inner pockets that stretched heavy with gold.

"Aye, and might ye carry some of me dowry in yer sporran? To lessen the weight of me dress."

Once she was dressed, Huey turned his attention back to the fire and made a torch out of a thick piece of wood. "We'll use this to start a fire at the shelter I saw. And then I'll find us somethin' to eat."

***

NIGHT FELL, AND with it came a bone-deep cold that sent shivers through their weary bodies. They huddled together in the shelter, their breath forming misty clouds in the crisp air.

They'd had a supper of mushrooms Huey found, but their thirst was not abated.

Dawn came as early as the day before. Huey woke with the lass in his arms. Despite the situation, he smiled and lay still until she woke.

While Rhona took a moment to herself behind the bothan, Huey started carving a point into the end of a thick stick. He wanted a weapon, if he couldn't have a sword or a pistol, then a spear would have to do. He had no idea if the area held wild animals, or worse—Englishmen.

Rhona came back around and they decided on a direction. The rugged terrain of the unknown land stretched out before them as they trekked northward, their eyes constantly scanning the horizon. From time to time Rhona called out for Mairi and Huey lifted his voice to summon the ghillie. They were not answered.

Their clothes had dried, but the journey became more arduous as they moved further inland, away from the shore.

"Do ye think we're in England?" Rhona's steps slowed.

Huey paused and glanced around at the rolling hills. "We came through a dense forest and these hills look as though they might favor heather in the spring. It's hard to say, lass. 'Tis a familiar feeling I have lookin' aboot. Mayhaps we be in a remote part of our homeland. We'll keep heading north until we find people. Their reaction to us will tell us what we need to ken."

"I've been lookin' aboot fer signs of fairies and I havena seen any." Rhona sighed and Huey laughed. "Ye doan believe in the wee folk?"

"Aye … wee they be … like mice what snatch the crumbs."

"God made giants like Goliath. Surely He could make a fairy."

Huey nodded and smiled. "Call out to them, then. Fer help."

"I will then." Rhona looked in all directions then focused on the path they'd just climbed up. Looking down it she yelled, "Hey-o! Can ye help us?"

A faint response, not an echo, met her ears. Huey, wide-eyed, grabbed her arm to stop her from yelling again. He took a deep breath and shouted out, "Who be there? Friend or foe?"

There was a pause in the very air itself and then an answer came in a loud and masculine voice: "Friend!"

A rustle, running feet, and then emerging from the lower path came three bedraggled figures. Donnie first and then Mairi, and following with a limp came Esmeralda.

"A skilled tracker, ye surely be," Huey praised Donnie, grabbing his hand to shake, and noticing the still tight grip the man had on his sack of treasure.

Rhona enfolded Mairi into her embrace and the two women wept for joy. Esmeralda stood mutely observing, black braids trembling on her shoulders. The happy reunion was then tempered by the Spanish woman's glare.

"Are we to believe no sailor rescued the captain?" Rhona gasped.

"*Los marineros son diablos*. Devils they are. I made it to shore inside the very barrel my Ian shoved me in. Once ashore my screams brought seamen who pulled the lid off and stole my treasures and left me to mourn in the sand. Alone."

"Aye," Donnie finished for her, "we found her keenin' on the beach. The captain must have drowned. We couldna leave her to fend fer herself when her own crew abandoned her."

Mairi put an arm around the widow and said, "'Twill be all right, mistress. We'll still find ye a way to Spain."

"Aye, we will." To Rhona and Huey, Donnie said, "She's promised us a place in her royal family's estate."

Rhona frowned and glanced at Esmeralda, then said to Donnie, "She told me all her family was lost at sea long ago."

Donnie shook his head. "I'm nay so good at readin' lies on ladies' faces. At least we dinnae waste our time goin' south. Fer Mairi's sake I followed yer tracks. I spotted the place ye burnt the driftwood and found the bothan, too. The master's boots and yer small shoes made fer easy trackin'."

"Ye must be hungry," Huey said. He reached into his sporran and brought out a handful of mushrooms. "I was savin' these, but ye can have 'em."

Esmeralda raised a haughty eyebrow and shook her head.

"'Tis all right," Mairi stated. "Me Donnie trapped two rabbits and roasted them fer our breakfast. I was smart to wed a ghillie."

There was little else to speak of but to agree on continuing the journey northward. Donnie took the lead, insisting that his skills would get them to a road or town or castle faster.

He was nearly right. Eventually, his efforts led them to a modest farm nestled in a peaceful valley. A kind man, Eamon Montgomery, welcomed them, offering water, food, and a place to rest in his barn.

As they sat around the man's hearth, savoring a simple meal, Eamon listened to their tale of the shipwreck and their uncertain journey. After a thoughtful pause, Eamon spoke in a reassuring voice, "Ye are indeed in Scotland, me friends. And if ye wish to find yer way home, ye must follow the road west. It'll take ye to Killearn. Go then north or jog south to the port what brings us goods from England. Ye might catch a frigate north."

Rhona shook her head violently. "I'll nay set foot on another sea-goin' vessel in me life."

"Nor I," agreed Mairi.

Esmeralda sucked in a stuttering breath, but said nothing.

"Of course," the farmer said, "I'd nay be unwelcomin' of a helpin' hand if any of ye wish to stay …" He smiled at Esmeralda.

Later, in the barn, Mairi and Donnie spoke quietly to Rhona and Huey. "We've been thinkin', maybe we should cross into England instead and hide there for but a wee while," Donnie suggested.

Huey exchanged a meaningful look with Rhona. The idea of returning to their clans was both comforting and terrifying, but he thought it might be best, though the memory of Hamish's pursuit haunted him as much as the fiery nightmare of the shipwreck.

"Perhaps 'tis best fer ye two," Huey said, "but I intend to take me lady home and wed her proper-like in a wee kirk the Beldorneys attend."

"'Tis decided then," Donnie said. "Our paths will split. We'll seek refuge in the land of the Sassenachs. And the captain's wife may come with us." He looked around. "Where be the woman?"

Mairi chuckled. "She's made a different choice, I believe. She's in the farmer's … care."

Chapter 10

HAMISH KILMAHEW HAD ridden hard and fast in pursuit of the *Sea Serpent*. He had hoped to reach a southern port and secure passage to Spain, where he believed the ship would be making landfall. His obsession with vengeance had consumed him, and he cared not for the dangers that might lie ahead.

As he reached the first Scottish port south of Yarwold, his heart sank at the news that met him. A fierce storm, one he had not encountered on his wild ride, had ravaged the seas. He learned from the dock workers there that a single seaman had survived and was spreading the tale and telling of riches to be found where the *Sea Serpent*'s anchor lay beneath the waves. Hamish found the man and bought him a strong drink. The sailor had little else to tell of the captain or crew and the few passengers; all, he claimed, were lost to the depths.

The ship Hamish had pursued with such determination had met a tragic end. There were no other survivors, the seaman insisted as he eyed Hamish's fine clothes.

Anger and disappointment coursed through Hamish, though not grief. He left the pub and looked out at the sea. His dream of having Rhona Kilmahew had been dashed, and his relentless pursuit had been in vain. There'd be no vengeance now. Nor pleasure.

He mounted his weary horse and began the long ride home, passing through the small town of Killearn on his way. The sight of the bustling town and the people going about their daily lives grated on his nerves. He needed a strong drink himself and perhaps a game of cards. He wouldn't go back completely empty-handed.

***

IT WAS AN emotional good-bye for Rhona and Mairi, but once she released her maid, Rhona tucked her arm in Huey's and didn't look back.

They walked for hours until they heard the noise.

The small town of Killearn was lively and they passed many Scottish folk as they made their way through its cobbled streets. In their disheveled state they garnered a few stares. Had they been dressed and coifed as elegantly as they were used to, they might have caused a bit of talk. They approached the modest inn near the center of the town, where Huey hoped to hire a coach to take them to Beldorney Hall. There they could bathe and press his grandparents for fresh clothing before going on to their planned stops: the kirk, his farm, and finally to Kilmahew Castle. Rhona had modestly assured him on the walk that once properly wed, her mother and father would accept them.

"Och, ye're in luck," said the burly innkeeper when Huey inquired, "me nephew's coach is pullin' up jist now and headin' north, he is. Ye doan look like ye can afford the fare, though." He named a price higher than Huey expected. He gave the innkeeper a disappointed look.

"'Twill be a hardship, fer sure." He hesitated to open his sporran in front of anyone and reveal the considerable number of gold coins he had. "Thank ye, sir." He turned and put his arm around Rhona to walk out as if they were in deep conversation about the sacrifice they must make to pay such a fare. Once outside, he retrieved the amount they needed, and walked up to the carriage. It looked to be a sturdy coach, its horses harnessed and ready to go. They found the driver running a hand down one horse's leg, and spoke to him.

"Are ye the innkeeper's nephew?"

"Aye, I am," he answered, straightening.

"De ye have room aboard for us?"

"Aye." He named a price half of what the innkeeper had said. Huey, jaw tight, handed the money over to him.

The driver, a young man with a pleasant face, nodded as he took the coins and let his gaze linger long on Rhona. Huey returned the extra coins to his sporran, quickly helped Rhona up into the coach, and then followed suit, his heart a smidgen lighter with the anticipation of heading home.

***

HAMISH RODE THROUGH the town square, his eyes wide with shock. There, about to step into a waiting carriage, were Rhona and that scoundrel who kidnapped her. Rhona's face turned away to look where she was stepping; she hadn't seen him. Huey's expression was that of a tired traveler. Of course it was; they'd survived a shipwreck and traveled all this way on foot. *Did the lad see him? No.* Hamish's heart pounded as he watched them, his hatred for Huey intensifying. They were on the brink of escaping his grasp once again, but that wasn't going to happen. For a moment he considered confronting them now, but wouldn't it be easier to follow and catch them unaware away from prying eyes? And if they were heading north, all the better. It would save him the cost of hiring a coach for her or buying her a horse and saddle to ride the distance.

He glared at the carriage door as it closed, then quickly turned his horse so as not to be seen through the window. That Beldorney lad had just seen the last of the sun. He'd be dead by nightfall, shot or stabbed or skewered by Hamish; he hadn't decided how he'd do the deed yet, but the thought of it gave him renewed energy. *Perhaps the cross bow, for a silent death.*

***

RHONA STARTLED SLIGHTLY as the carriage door opened again and two men bent to enter. Quick and curt introductions were made. The older of the two, James Glencairn, was a middle-aged man with a stern countenance, dressed in the formal attire of a tax collector, which he was. His son, Jeremiah, was equally stiff and official-acting, a younger version of his father, whose eyes glanced often at Rhona, but whose hand never let go of the leather satchel at his side.

Rhona relaxed. She knew her place among men, though she felt naked without her bonnet and she blushed with embarrassment each time her gaze shyly flickered to the floor where her muddied shoes peeked from under the frazzled hem of her dress. The carriage jerked forward, then rumbled on at an even pace.

She'd heard her father and uncle speak often—and severely—about tax collectors. Her ears perked up as she listened to Glencairn teach his son about his unwelcome duties, patting the packet of parchments on his lap as he did. Their conversation revolved around the various taxes of the day. Glencairn, in a most authoritative tone, explained the nuances of the cart tax, the carriage tax, and the infamous window tax that had been a point of contention among many people.

With her hand linked under Huey's arm, Rhona felt his muscle tense at the discussion, but he and she kept silent.

"The window tax was implemented as a means intended to cover the cost of reminting damaged and clipped coinage," James Glencairn explained, his voice carrying a conceited air of authority. "The more windows, the more tax, favoring the poor, of course." He gave a snooty glance at Huey. "But many households simply brick up their windows to reduce what they owe. We must make careful inventory, ye see."

Rhona felt Huey tense more and then he leaned forward. She glanced at his face and saw the curiosity there.

"What about the farm horse tax, sir?" he asked.

Glencairn scrutinized Huey, his eyebrows raised in mild surprise at the interruption. Rhona had seen that look before; it was the same way a man looked at her, assessing if it was worth the time to explain something to a lowly woman who hadn't the wits to understand the simplest things. The tax collector must have deemed Huey bright enough. After a short hesitation, he responded.

"Ah … the farm horse tax … 'tis what we are workin' on now." He cleared his throat. "'Tis based on the number of horses a farmer has. 'Twill take us three months to visit twenty-nine parishes before finishing with the parish of Dumfries, but we'll have a number high into the thousands, I believe."

"And what does the government use the revenue fer?"

Before Glencairn could provide an answer, the carriage hit a rough patch of road, jostling them violently. The sudden jolt caused a loud snap and a lurch as the carriage came to an abrupt halt.

Rhona clung to Huey and she noticed Jeremiah grab his father's arm. The man shook him off, clutched his papers, and looked out the window.

He swore loudly. "We're stopped! Heaven help us if we've got ourselves a broken axle," he grumbled.

***

93

HAMISH CONTINUED TO follow the carriage at a cautious distance. His determination was unwavering, driven by the burning obsession to claim Rhona—*thank the stars she did not drown*—and exact revenge on Huey Beldorney—*damn the devil he did not drown.*

As he rode in silence, the distant sounds of the carriage stopping suddenly reached his ears—a sharp crack followed by shouts. The driver's profanity filled the air, and Hamish couldn't help but smile. Fate had intervened and granted him an opportunity.

He halted his horse a short distance away, his mind racing with new plans. Now would have to be the time to strike. If what he thought had happened—a broken axle—it would take the driver hours to fix it, if he could. The man might strand the passengers and take a horse back to town for supplies. Hamish could only hope that would be the case. Striking at dark would always be preferable. He glanced at the sky, the sun hanging low.

He dismounted, unlashed the crossbow tied to his saddle, took his rifle, too, and crept as close as he dared, keeping himself hidden from view by a thicket of trees.

***

JAMES GLENCAIRN GREW increasingly frustrated and anxious, nudging his son and whispering to him, "Keep a tight grip on that satchel. Ready yer pistol."

Huey tensed up. "What mean ye, sir?"

"There might be highwaymen awaitin' fer us. They dig pits in the road, cover'em with straw and when a carriage wheel breaks because of it, they attack." He peered out the window, a small pistol already in his hand.

Huey looked out the window on his side and reached for the door. "I'll see what the problem may be." He gave a nod to Rhona who shrank away from the window on her side.

"Lad," the tax collector said, "give a holler if ye see the bandits. I've had to shoot me fair share of men tryin' to do their own tax collectin'."

***

HAMISH SLIPPED THROUGH the brush, his movements silent, and positioned himself behind a large boulder from which he could take aim without being seen. He laid the rifle on the ground and steadied his breathing. His fingers deftly loaded a bolt into the crossbow, his heart

94

pounding with anticipation. The carriage door opened and Huey descended. *What luck!* He restrained his grin and steadied the crossbow, lining up the shot, waiting for the perfect moment. His finger caressed the crossbow's trigger.

And then, just as he released the bolt, fate intervened yet again. The carriage jolted forward a foot, Huey pitched head first, and tumbled, and the arrow that flew forth sped through the open door and pierced the flesh of a passenger within.

Anger gripped Hamish as he realized he now lost the element of surprise. He dropped the bow and grabbed the rifle.

***

RHONA'S SCREAM PIERCED the air like a whistle. The arrow had lanced through Glencairn's heart, pinning his body to the side of the carriage. His son shouted and panicked; he raised his pistol and began firing out the door. Huey stayed low on the ground, confused by the commotion, not understanding a silent arrow had whizzed past him as he'd fallen. His first thought was that the tax collector was shooting at him and intended to kill him, take his bride, and leave.

The carriage driver, too, had no idea what was transpiring. The firing of the gun startled the horses and since he had climbed down to check the axles, and not set the brake, the animals freely bolted. The carriage moved past, Huey near the front wheel on one side and the driver near the back wheel on the other side. With the jerking start, the younger Glencairn tumbled out the door which slammed shut as soon as the wheels hit another rut. He jumped up, gun in hand, and shouted, "Me father's been shot!"

Huey had no time to decipher the words, all he knew was that the carriage was racing away driverless and Rhona was inside. He scrambled to his feet and ran after it. The driver also pursued it. Neither registered the exchange of gunfire behind them as coming from distinctly different firearms.

"Whoa," the driver kept yelling, his strides now matching Huey's. The pair ran fast down the road, but the horses were faster.

***

RHONA FROZE, HER eyes fixated on James Glencairn, so recently alive, so presently still, a stream of dark red blood staining his fine clothes, his hands bouncing against his sides like thick ropes, his head nodding rhythmically, his eyes open but unseeing, the small pistol slipping to the floor.

She'd grabbed the leather clutching strap to keep from falling forward. *Why were the horses running? Why had the driver left Huey and Jeremiah behind?*

She wanted to scream again, but only whimpers found their way up her throat. Then she heard the shouts of whoa coming from behind the coach. The realization that no one was controlling the horses hit her like an unexpected whack from a drunken father.

***

HAMISH WAS STILL cursing himself when he raised the rifle to aim at Huey. Then another young man plunged from the carriage and shot into the brush around Hamish. He ducked and waited, then rose in time to see the carriage speeding off, two men in pursuit. The third, the one who'd fired at him, was still facing his way. The man saw Hamish and fired again. Hamish sighted on the man, pulled the trigger, and watched, satisfied, as the man collapsed.

He left his crossbow on the ground and hurried back to his horse. Four human legs were no match for four equine legs … and, he thought, the driver and that blasted Beldorney would be easy kills on the open road.

***

THE KILMAHEW BATTLE cry reached Huey's ears and though he was intensely absorbed in chasing the carriage and rescuing Rhona, a sixth sense made him turn his head and look. It was both the wrong thing to do and the right thing.

He realized how wrong it was the moment he recognized the man who had imprisoned him in the Kilmahew dungeon. Running at full tilt was not going to be enough to get away from this mad man who was pushing his horse to run him down while aiming a gun at him. A half second later it didn't matter because Huey instinctively swerved. His foot landed in a rut, and he went rolling to the ground.

It was the right thing because Hamish's horse shied violently away from trampling Huey, whose arms and legs were flailing like hummingbird wings as he rolled.

Everything muted. The sound of the carriage's wheels and the horses' hoof beats ahead receded. The yells of the driver faded. Even the

96

birdsong he wasn't aware of before lessened to nothing, or, perhaps the birds stopped singing entirely when the reluctant horse also swerved, broke an ankle and fell. The loathsome man on its back was not only crushed by the half-ton animal but hit his head on a rather hard, granular rock.

Huey was panting. The sound of his own breath was what he heard first, not the pained groan of the writhing horse.

He rose, looked up the road, looked back at Hamish. The man was so still. Huey hadn't seen a man die since the time of the plague.

He took a step, tested his limbs. He wasn't hurt badly, only bruised. And yet he seemed paralyzed. It was the pathetic whinny of the horse that brought him to his senses. He stepped off the road and into the grass where he picked up Hamish's rifle, put the horse out of its misery, and threw the weapon back down on the ground. He stared at Hamish's body and pondered the fate of the man's soul. He spoke the traditional graveside blessing and added, "I fergive ye and doan harbor ill feelin's toward ye." He shook his head and started jogging up the road, praying for Rhona's safety with every step.

Chapter 11

THE CARRIAGE LAY on its side, the horses tangled in their riggings, but not thrashing wildly. Rhona found herself in a peculiar position, her feet on the ground, but still inside the carriage. How could that be? Her head pounded and dizziness gripped her. Her back was against the ceiling of the coach and if she tried to stretch a bit she might be able to raise her head and … and …

She crumpled back into a ball, her left hand catching on something soft. Squishy. Warm. Wet. She turned her chin and looked at her shoulder, her eyes followed her sleeve down to her elbow, her wrist, her fingers. She gasped and drew back her hand as quickly as she could from the soft neck of James Glencairn.

Her mind was a moment behind in recognizing the fact she already knew: the man was dead. Shot through with an arrow. They'd raced away down the road. She'd screamed when the carriage took a turn too fast and rolled. A wave of calm washed over her for the single moment that things made sense. Of course that was the ground. The carriage was on its side. The door torn away. If she tried to stand, she'd be tall enough to pop up through the opposite side.

She looked up. Yes, the other door. The window. She glanced back at Glencairn and the panic returned. The world seemed to spin, and she felt a deep, gut-wrenching sorrow wash over her. Where was the driver? Where was the tax collector's son? Where, oh where, was Huey?

Suddenly the carriage rocked a bit.

"Are ye all right in there?" A voice, panting and faint, repeated the question. A shadow blocked what light was coming in above and a face appeared. It was the driver. "Och, ye're hurt. Raise a hand. I'll pull ye out."

His words were muffled by the ringing in her ears, but his gestures were clear—he was offering to help her. She reached up, unsteady, but once his hand gripped her wrist, it was obvious she'd have to step on the dead man's body to climb out, a horrifying reality.

"Nay, nay," she whispered to herself, her chest tightening, "I'll nay think on it." She closed her eyes and let him pull her up, scraping parts of her as he did so. The driver put an arm around her waist and finished the extraction, his hands dangerously near her bosom. The thought raced through her mind that she did not even know this man's name.

He carried her and walked a ways from the wreckage. She kept her eyes shut until he spoke again.

"Can ye stand?" He set her feet on the roadside grass and she clutched at him for balance. "Ye can sit then." He knelt with her and set her on the ground. "Are ye all right? I need to see to me horses."

She opened her eyes then and focused on his face. He was looking at the animals. She followed his gaze and saw the poor beasts snorting and struggling against their riggings, the carriage lying before them on its side, looking like some giant had kicked it over and pulled its wheels off.

The driver began to rise and Rhona snagged his sleeve. "Wait … he's dead … the passenger."

"Aye, I saw him. And the other two are missin'." He looked down the road. "I'll settle down me horses and then go in search of them."

"He thought there were highwaymen. He had a pistol. They both did."

The driver frowned. "Who?"

"The dead man. The tax collector."

"Is the pistol still in there? I should get it. The highwaymen are sure to follow."He swore lightly under his breath. "Me rifle fell from the coach. A pistol will have to do." He grunted and rose, strode back to the carriage and climbed up its belly.

Rhona watched, clutching her arms around herself and beginning to shake. Her head still pounded and various muscles started to twitch.

Little vocal sounds escaped her throat in short hiccups, as if she found it funny to see the driver's boots flailing for balance as he tipped himself upside down to hunt for the pistol.

She wanted to cry, but she couldn't. Maybe she should laugh. Or shout. Call out for Huey. Yes, that was what she needed to do. Wobbling, she rose, took a few steps toward the road and looked both ways. She wasn't sure from which direction they had come. "Huey?" His name came out of her mouth as soft as a fairy's whisper. She collapsed to her knees and then … blackness.

***

HUEY'S STRONG ARMS were wrapped around her. She was sure they were his arms. She opened her eyes and for a brief moment found comfort in his embrace. His voice was a soothing balm, reassuring her that she was safe and uninjured.

"Oh, praise be," his voice was suddenly louder, "ye're awake at last."

"Did I faint? Oh, ye came." She looked about. One horse was gone, the other tied to a tree.

"Aye. I came runnin'. The driver was tendin' to ye, almost shot me till he recognized me."

"Where did he go?"

"On ahead. To get help. And shovels."

"Shovels?"

"Aye, we've a bit of a problem." He nodded toward the carriage. "That Glencairn fellow is dead and so's his son. And … another … down the road."

"A highwayman?" Rhona stiffened and turned herself to face Huey, her legs across his as she sat in his lap on the ground.

"Nay, someone worse than a highwayman. 'Twas yer uncle."

Rhona gasped. "And he's … dead?"

"Aye."

"Ye killt him?"

"Nay. He chased after us. Woulda killt me, but his horse stumbled … he was crushed when they fell, hit his head on a rock. I'll go back and bury him fer ye … ye can say a prayer."

***

THE DRIVER, WHOSE name they finally learned was Theo Gilchrist, returned at dusk with another carriage and a second man—the town's

100

undertaker—who brought a wagon. Theo tied the extra horse to the wagon and lashed the tax collector's body over it. There was quite a bit of money in the dead man's satchel. Enough, Theo said, to pay for the repairs to his carriage, pay the undertaker to collect the other two bodies and bury all three dead men in the next town.

Rhona whispered to Huey that she did not want to see her uncle's body. Huey spoke privately to Theo and it was agreed—with a few more coins from Huey's sporran—that Theo would take them immediately to an inn and leave the clean-up to the undertaker.

Rhona breathed easier and endured the bumpy ride to the inn snuggled against Huey.

"We'll get ye a new dress in the morn and travel on," Huey said. "Do ye still have yer dowry in yer pockets?"

In the dark of the carriage Rhona ran her fingers along her hips and felt the knotted kerchiefs still sheltering the gold and silver and jewels. "Aye. I was ready to spend it all on goin' to America or Spain or wherever we might go. Now I'm hopin' that with Hamish gone, me father will relent when he learns how McDoon and his own brother meant to abuse me. We can use the dowry fer yer farm and I'll nay have to be so far from me mum."

"I'll remind yer father of our wager. We played a game of chess fer yer hand in marriage. I was on the verge of claimin' ye when Hamish burst in and took me to the dungeon. If yer father be a fair man, he'll let me face him in another game. I've nay doubt I can win."

"But me father is a shrewd man. He'll make ye stake somethin' more … yer fortune … yer farm."

Huey lifted her chin with his hand and stared into her eyes. "Ye are me fortune. All I want is ye by me side … forever." He kissed her gently and held her close. His fingers caressed her shoulders, her cheeks, her hair, and then he ran his hands down her sides and lifted her to sit upon his lap. They ignored the jostles and bumps and ruts and kept their lips and tongues busy—kissing, whispering, loving.

***

THE INNKEEPER HAD no rooms and Theo, confessing that the tax collector's funds were "a wee bit more than necessary fer an honest man," offered to drive on through the night to get them to Beldorney Hall.

Huey's grandmother, Baroness Beldorney, was ecstatic to see the bedraggled pair arrive the next morning.

She ordered three maids to tend to Rhona and had a second bath drawn for her grandson. The maids dashed off with their charge, chattering about which dresses in the guest wardrobe might fit her.

While waiting for the heated water to be brought to Huey's usual room, the Baroness made him sit before the hearth, asked him to explain his presence fully, and listened intently to his tale. Servants brought steaming buckets of water, one by one, as he related how he met Rhona while hunting, courted her secretly, played chess for her hand, was imprisoned, escaped, and fled with her and two servants.

His grandmother smiled at first, looked scared in parts, and clapped when he told of surviving the ship wreck. The last of the hot water was delivered and a servant brought a fresh set of clothes, laying them on the bed about the time Huey was describing the runaway carriage. The servant lingered, tending the fire, and then standing by the tub ready to assist the young Beldorney heir.

Huey finished the account and his grandmother said, "A taller tale I've never heard. I'll be sure to repeat the best parts of the story to the Baron when he wakes. He sleeps most of the day and frets all of the night."

Huey sighed. "Ye told me before ye dinnae think he'd see the spring."

"The doctor, the one what traveled through here last week, claimed he had more life than that. He believed a season of withholding his ale and whiskey would give him several years more of life. A doctor Muir, it was. A kind gentleman."

Huey laughed then. "I remember him. Did ye ken his daughter married Colin McKelvey? She was the apothecary in Yarwold, who helped us sneak onto the ship." He shook his head and stood, eyeing the steam from the tub. "I cannae see me *seanathair* givin' up the strong drink willingly. Nay wonder he frets all night."

His grandmother nodded and smiled. "I'll let ye get to yer bath. Then ye must tell me more of this Kilmahew lass. When do ye plan to wed her?" She rose too.

"I thought we might engage the vicar at yer kirk and marry today, but …"

"Oh, no, no, no," the Baroness said, reverting to the English accent of her youth, "I did not approve when your father married Fenella and we suffered a rift between us until you were born. I'm sorry we didn't bless their union as we did my daughter's. Please give Rhona's mother the chance to see her daughter wed."

Huey took his grandmother's hands in his and kissed her knuckles. "I'll take yer wise advice."

She gave him a quick hug and left the room. Huey began to undress.

***

RHONA HAD FOLLOWED the maids into the bed chamber tired from her long and eventful journey. The prospect of a hot bath was especially inviting since she hadn't had one in so long. The room's draperies were closed against the early morning's sunrise, which was fine with her as she was exhausted and if the Baroness hadn't suggested a bath, she would have been equally happy with simply lying down on a soft mattress. The warm glow of candles were easier on her eyes.

Her footsteps echoed softly on the polished stone floor, then muted as she stepped onto the rug beside the copper tub. Her shoes were embarrassingly dirty. She sat on the chair and before she could bend to remove them, one of the cheery maids knelt in front of her and did this service for her.

"Thank ye," Rhona sighed. "I'm sorry, I dinnae hear yer names."

"I'm Rosalie," the girl said. "These be me sisters, Nell and Fiona. Maids in trainin' ye might say. They came to Beldorney Hall this summer after the games when the Fraser twins chose other lasses fer brides."

Rhona glanced at the girls, their faces showing no shame from their sister's revelation, rather their charming countenances were flushed with the excitement of having a young lady to wait on.

Nell curtsied. "Pleased to meet ye, m'lady." And Fiona shyly smiled and poured a bucket of steaming water into the tub. She rushed out of the room, undoubtedly to fetch more from the kitchen. It was a challenging duty to haul water from a well, and more so to heat it up and lug it up the stairs all for the benefit of a high-born lady or gent. Rhona was grateful and momentarily missed her maid, Mairi. She wished she'd express her gratitude more often for all Mairi had done for her. She wondered if she'd ever see her again.

103

Rosalie and Nell began to chatter away like a pair of sparrows, their voices rising and falling in melody as one combed out the snarls in Rhona's hair and the other worked on the buttons on her dress.

"Yer hair, m'lady," Nell said, her cheeks dimpling as she spoke, "'tis like a cascade o' fine bronze-colored silk. We shall style it so beautifully; the Baroness will be envious."

Rosalie finished with the buttons. "If ye're done wi' the combin', Rosalie, help me get this dress off her."

"'Tis heavy, indeed." Nell frowned. "What be in the pockets?"

"Oh," Rhona sighed, "'tis me dowry. A small part of the Kilmahew fortune, I suppose."

Rosalie and Nell both gasped. "Ye're a Kilmahew?" The lasses' infectious energy lagged and they tried their best to hide their feelings.

"What's wrong?" Rhona stepped out of the dress and stood there in her shift.

"Nary a thing, m'lady."

Fiona thrust the door open and spoke to someone in the hall. She tottered in with a heavy bucket. "There's another in the hall. The steward brought it up for Master Huey, but I convinced him to leave it for the Mistress here. He'll have to get another. Can ye fetch it, Nell?"

"Aye."

Fiona smiled at Rhona as she emptied the water into the tub, but her face changed when she caught the looks on her sisters' faces. "What happened? Did someone die?"

Rhona touched the edge of the tub. "I'm a Kilmahew and it seems the name disgusts yer sisters."

"Oh, nay, nay, m'lady," Rosalie protested. "'Tis only that … well … our mother … she speaks well of every clan … except the name Hamish Kilmahew sends her into paroxysms of grief and anger. 'Tis a long story."

"I can imagine," Rhona said. The last bucket was sloshed into the tub and Rhona lifted a leg to test the temperature with her toe. "But ye can tell yer mum the man is dead. He cracked his skull on a rock jist yesterday."

The mood in the room changed as suddenly as before and the maids resumed their happy jabber without so much as a comment on the man's misfortune. Fiona took a bouquet of lavender from a basket by the tub and began crushing pieces of it into the tub.

"Here, Mistress Rhona, we have the most fragrant herbs fer yer bath. Lavender to relax ye, rosemary to raise yer spirits, and mint to refresh ye."

Rosalie chirped, "The young master willna resist ye as ye fill his eyes with beauty and his nose with these perfumes."

Nell gathered the travel-stained clothes and asked, "M'lady ... aboot yer dowry ... I'll set the coins upon yon table and fetch ye a proper lady's bag fer them."

"Thank ye, Nell." Rhona slipped further into the tub. Her shift floated around her, still allowing for a modicum of modesty, but once she was fully submerged and the flower petals blanketed the water's surface, she pulled the sopping garment up and over her head. Nell took it and stuffed it into one of the buckets.

Rosalie handed Rhona a scrubbing brush and fine scented soap. "M'lady, have ye heard? The Baroness has offered ye the pick of the gowns. The finest silks and laces."

Nell nodded eagerly, "And stockings and slippers and hair fobs and jewels. A treasure trove, to be sure."

Fiona chimed in with, "Once ye're all clean and pampered, we'll make sure yer skin glows like moonlight. The Baroness has the finest oils and lotions."

Rhona sank further, enjoying the luxury, feeling all the tension and grime of the journey wash away. The maids continued to prattle on about fashion and the fine meal cook was preparing and ... she heard no more as she held her breath and dipped under. When she came up, Nell took to lathering up her hair. Fiona left to get a final bucket for rinsing and Rosalie began to lay out a selection of undergarments.

***

HUEY STOOD IN the opulent room where his grandmother sat doing her embroidering. Fine tapestries draped the walls and expensive furnishings filled the room. A crackling fire of cedar logs warmed the room and autumn daylight streamed through the tall windows. Huey spotted the old chess set of the Baron's, lavish pieces carved of ebony and boxwood.

"Ye look fine, indeed," the Baroness said, approving of the white shirt and stockings and the fresh kilt in the rich tartan pattern of the Beldorney clan's colors. "Come sit next to me. The maid expects the lass to be presentable in half an hour or so. Her hair is still wet it seems."

Huey's lips curled at the mention of Rhona. He was looking forward to presenting her again to his grandmother, but in a more formal way.

The Baroness set down her work and asked, "Did ye get the pastries I had sent to yer rooms to ease yer hunger pains a bit? There's bein' fixed a fine noon meal fer ye."

"Aye. And thank ye fer these clothes."

"'Tis nothin'."

The door swung open and a pert maid announced Rhona. Rhona stepped forward and Huey's jaw dropped. She was a vision of grace and beauty. For a moment he felt unworthy of the radiant lass before him. It wasn't the gown she wore, a masterpiece of silk and lace that flowed like a waterfall of elegance to the floor. It wasn't the set of pearls around her neck that shimmered in the morning light. It wasn't the tiara that glittered and threatened to tip from her shining locks. None of those things mattered to him. It was the look she was giving him. He was struck by her bright countenance, her eyes that sparkled with excitement, and her smile, meant only to warm his heart. Love. Pure love. He knew it, felt it, saw it. He rushed to her side and put her hand on his arm to escort her into the room.

The delicate scent of lavender and rosemary clung to her. He wanted to speak, to tell her how beautiful she looked, but his tongue wouldn't loosen.

He brought her toward his grandmother. Finally, breaking the silence, he cleared his throat and wakened his tongue. "Grandmother, this is Rhona Kilmahew. Rhona, this be me grandmother, the Baroness Beldorney."

Rhona curtsied gracefully. "'Tis a pleasure to meet ye ... again ..." She smiled and the Baroness reached for her hand and tugged her toward the seat Huey had so recently vacated.

"Sit by me, dear."

Huey took a side chair and scooted it to angle toward them both. He could see his grandmother's approval; Rhona's instant charm had won her over, now that she was more presentable.

"The pleasure is mine, Rhona. Huey has told me the tale of yer adventure. I wish to play a wee part in yer story. There was once a secret princess that came here ..." Huey's grandmother continued with the story of his Aunt Eleanor and Uncle Keir. He was a young lad at the time and only remembered how Keir had let him hold the heavy claymore sword. "... and so," she concluded ten minutes later, "they were married at Castle Caladh. But I've always wished such a grand and elegant wedding could take place here."

During her lengthy narrative Huey had paid more attention to Rhona, letting his thoughts go to their future, absorbed in admiration of his intended bride. But he snapped to the present when his grandmother expressed her wish.

"*Seanmhair,* ye needna make such a generous offer."

"Baroness," Rhona nodded her head, the tiara in danger of tipping, "we thank ye with grateful hearts. 'Tis generous, indeed, as Huey says, but ..."

"Oh, I understand, ye want yer mother at the doin's. I told Huey this morn that ye shouldna wed without her as a witness. But I thought we could send a carriage for them. Yer father, Laird Kilmahew, has tried fer twenty years to get an invitation here. I'll now grant him one. They willna protest yer marriage if 'tis to be performed at Beldorney Hall."

Rhona looked at Huey, one hand gently pushing the tiara back in place.

With one voice they agreed.

"Wonderful," the Baroness said. Her eyes were moist. "Now, I have somethin' else." She reached for a small, velvet-lined box on a nearby table. She opened it to reveal a necklace of exquisite craftsmanship: a delicate chain of gold from which hung a sapphire large enough to reflect the depths of the ocean. "For you, my dear," she said in perfect English. "It was a gift from the royal family. Once upon a time I was admitted to court."

"Thank ye," Rhona said. Huey could detect the emotion in her voice.

Chapter 12

THE WEDDING DATE was set for ten days hence, enough time to inform the Kilmahews, the McKelveys, the Carlyles, and various other clans. As the special day approached, a wave of excitement swept through the Highlands. There was much speculation about how the joining of two rival clans came about, but the rumors that traveled the countryside leaned toward more positive conjectures: love, harmony, unity.

It was to be a grand celebration at Beldorney Hall. Huey's father and sister arrived two days in advanced, followed thereafter by friends and family and, on the day of the wedding, Rhona's mother and father stepped off their carriage a mere hour before the appointed time, heads held high and manners in check.

They were escorted to the best seats in the large ballroom, which had been transformed into a sanctuary of sorts, decorated with tartan ribbons and heather wreaths. Banners of every attending clan hung on the stone walls. Laird Kilmahew, like the rest of the men, wore a kilt; his wife, Cait, looked as pretty as the bride, wearing a gown splendidly adorned with lace and jewels. A plumed hat for her, a gold kilt brooch for him, added more elegance.

The Lady Kilmahew also had a sly smirk upon her face, as if she, too, might slip away when the bride and groom did, a hidden treasure strapped to her thighs and an escape plan to execute once her husband over-indulged in the wedding feast's grand selection of wines.

Gifts for the bride and groom piled up in the grand hall. Elaborate boxes containing jewelry, family heirlooms, and even finely crafted swords were presented with pride. Guests uttered blessings with each offering, creating an atmosphere of reverence and camaraderie. There was peace in the Highlands.

Once all were seated, Huey strode to the front, handsome in his family's tartan, his face shaved, his hair pulled back and bound with a special ribbon, a grin never leaving his face. He addressed everyone.

"When I first met Rhona Kilmahew, I was charmed not only by her beauty and grace, her kindness and her artistic talent, but by something else that radiated from within her. Ye've heard the tales, I'm sure, of our elopement, foiled at every turn. Pursued, shipwrecked, and very nearly killed. But with each trial and tribulation we grew closer. I stand before ye today to declare me love fer the lass, a love that goes beyond stormy seas, pitted roads, dungeons, and," he glanced at Brian Kilmahew, "clan feuds and enmity. May the Beldorneys, the McKelveys, the Kilmahews, and every clan represented here today, be forever united in peace." He nodded to the musician at the door. The bagpiper took a deep breath and started the expected tune.

The vicar walked up to the wedding arch that had been built for the occasion. Brian Kilmahew stood and bowed to Huey, then walked purposefully to the door where Rhona stood, took her hand, and brought her forward for the ceremony.

When the melody ended Keir McKelvey whispered to his wife, "Och, 'tis a splendid day. Wee Huey has become quite a man. I think he might even love his wife as much as I love mine." He smiled at her, squeezed her hand, and looked down their row at the faces of his children. His son was still a lad, but his daughters were of age. There'd be betrothals to arrange in the coming year.

Eleanor patted his hand and smirked. She put a finger to her lips and raised an eyebrow at her husband. Behind her she could hear Hannah's husband, Logan, whispering a similar sweet remark to her good friend. There were other soft voices echoing in the large room, but all went silent when the vicar cleared his throat.

The words of the ceremony, spoken in Gaelic and then repeated in English, filled the room with solemnity and a good bit of joy. Soon there'd be a feast. It was already set in the grand dining hall. There tables groaned with the weight of platters laden with roasted meats and savory pies. The aromas could not be denied; they filled the air even here in the ballroom.

And before the sun set, there'd be dancing and reveling, fiddlers and flutes, and merriment until the wee hours. Torches would be lit, candle chandeliers would flicker golden light that would enhance the blushing cheeks of women, young and old.

But first, the wedding. The ancient vows were spoken, the vicar made his pronouncement, and Huey embraced his bride. Neither cared that so many were watching their intimate moment. He pulled her tight against him. The kiss went on and on while men cheered, cousins laughed, and women's hearts fluttered.

The Highlander's Forbidden Love

Made in the USA
Middletown, DE
29 May 2024

55033848R00066